MW00932267

CHRISTMAS IN CRISIS

AN OLYMPIA BROWN MYSTERY

JUDITH CAMPBELL

FINE.LINE.PRESS

~Fine.Line.Press~
All rights reserved

Names, characters and incidents depicted in this book are products of the
author's imagination or are used fictitiously or with permission. Any
resemblance to actual events, organizations, or persons, living or dead, is
purely coincidental and beyond the intent of the author or the publisher.

No part of this book may be reproduced or transmitted in any form or by
any means, electronic or mechanical including photocopying recording or by
any information storage and retrieval system without permission in writing
from the author.

Copyright 2017, by Judith Campbell
ISBN-13: 978-1979987066
ISBN-10:1979987068

Published in the United States of America
~Fine.Line.Press~

FOREWORD

Sanctuary Knocker, 1300, CE
Durham Cathedral, County Durham, England

The knocker on Durham Cathedral's northern door is known
as the Sanctuary Knocker. It played an important part in the

[Durham, UK] cathedral's history. Those who "had committed a great offence," such as murder in self-defense or breaking out of prison, could rap the knocker, and would be given 37 days of sanctuary within which they could try to reconcile with their enemies or plan their escape.

Sanctuary, noun; a place of refuge or safety.
Sanctuary | Sanctuary Definition by Merriam-Webster
a place where someone or something is protected or given shelter

To: Judi Ivie, Pamela Kelley, Karen Allen, editor extraordinaire, Chris/Frederick, 3 on 3 writers, OB writers, Jennifer, Ian, Colin, Liz, Laura, Leah, Anna, Melissa, Spencer, Erica, Monica, Lynda, Mhari, Jay, Karen, John, Marilyn, Bill, Giggleswick writers, Louise, Steve, Nikki, Gillian, Michael, Julie, David, Frimma, George, Maxi, Uncle Bill and Aunt Joan, Cousin Karen, Nancy and Elliott, Rebecca…et al, in other words, ….my characters, my inspiration and my literal and spiritual editors and on down days, my care and courage givers. Thank you.

PREFACE

"In the bleak midwinter, frosty wind made moan, earth stood hard as iron, water like a stone..." These words continue to trouble my thinking. Such a sad song for such a happy season. Perhaps, it is calling us to look deeper, to look behind the candles and merriment. There is much to ponder in this plaintive melody, as no doubt, I will.

More anon...

1

Emilio Vieira waited for a full ten minutes in the shadows behind the massive oak tree overhanging the church parking lot. He needed to make sure there was no one who might see him there and ask questions, or worse, call the police. When he was convinced he was safe, he walked quickly to the green back door of the old church and reached behind a cement planter for the plastic bag containing the key. After unlocking the door, he returned the bag and the key to their hiding place and slipped silently inside the dark empty building. Now, daring to breathe normally again, he turned and snapped the safety latch back into place. If things continued to work according to plan, he'd go and have a key made for himself. But not yet. He'd practiced letting himself in and out of the building several times without being seen. This time, he would stay the night. Only then would he make himself a key.

He'd been working on the logistics of this for weeks, and tonight, he would learn whether or not the final implementation was actually going to work. In the dark interior of the building, he moved slowly and carefully along the route he'd long since memorized. Without making a sound, he walked across the corridor, down the stairs, and through the children's area to where an old, creaky door opened into a long-unused dirt cellar. Here was the original foundation and very oldest part of the historic New England church. According to his research, this part of the structure dated all the way back to the church's construction in 1789. It smelled old and forgotten. He hoped and prayed it would remain that way.

Shutting the door and using his cell phone for light, he made his way across the uneven floor to where another staircase, long unused and even more forgotten, had once ascended to the sanctuary. Years ago, it had been permanently walled off at the top, and like the crawlspace, it was ancient history. A stairway to nowhere. For years, no one other than workmen, plumbers, or electricians had gone into that part of the building.

Originally, this was where the colonists who'd built the original church structure fled to hide from Indian raiders. Later in the history of the congregation, it became a place for abolitionist members of the church to hide runaway slaves. The church had a long history of providing safe sanctuary to those who needed it, and present-day members remained justly proud of that history.

He'd learned of all of this by poring over dusty, faded records and drawings in the library and town hall. He further expanded his knowledge of the place by attending a few Sunday services and having coffee in the parish social hall and meeting some of the congregation. But after the ritual newcomer greetings—"Welcome…what did you say your name was? Here, let me get you some coffee and something to eat. Uh, I'm sorry, what did you say your name was?" — they would smile and turn back to their friends. That never bothered Emilio. He wasn't there to make connections. He was engaged in personal research.

He used the pretext of trips to the men's room to check out and memorize the layout of the facility. He located the bathrooms, both upstairs and down, the kitchen, and the social and educational spaces. When well-intentioned people persisted, asking his name and where he came from and where he lived, he would only give them his first name, Emilio, that he was from Brazil, and that he worked in a local restaurant. This would usually suffice. If further pressed, he'd say only that he and a couple of guys had a place in Hull, a nearby and considerably less pricey town on the Southeastern Massachusetts coast.

With his first New England winter approaching, he needed to find a safe, dry place to sleep. Renting a room cost money, and he was sending almost all of what he made home to his family. He'd pretty much used up the charity and hospitality of his friends. Camping in a nearby state forest had served him well over the summer but with the shorter, colder days approaching, this would soon no longer be an option. He needed a warm, secure, permanent shelter, and he didn't have much time left to find it.

Now, safely inside and standing next to the forgotten stairway, he knew part one of his plan was accomplished. Alone in the semi-darkness, he located the moveable panel that edged the underside of the stairs and began to work it open. The old wood groaned and complained but eventually gave way to the pressure of his fingers, revealing another space. This was smaller and lower than the one he stood in. The dimensions were such that he could just about stand upright, stretch out his arms, and take a few steps in either direction. There was room enough to spread out his sleeping bag and still have space on the floor for his backpack and those few things he kept in his locker at work.

He looked around, no longer afraid to shine his light, and wondered if it would stay dry in a heavy rain. It didn't smell musty...just old and long empty. If he could find a way to dispose of some of the ancient clutter, he might be able to create a little more space where he might put something to sit on. Then maybe he'd look for an old milk crate or orange box where he could set out the picture of his daughter and mother. He let out a sigh of cautious relief, thinking of the tiny, brown-eyed baby he'd left behind. He watched her growing on Facebook and talked to her on Skype, but it was not the same as holding her, smelling her hair, and tickling her little toes. One day, he promised… But he was getting much too far ahead of himself. He would allow himself to think that he might have finally found himself a safe place. That was enough for now.

If his plans and calculations continued to work, he could sleep there undetected, use the bathrooms and sleep in the warmth of the nearby furnace. He could even recharge his phone and tap into the church Wi-Fi. He wouldn't use much of anything, and he'd never leave a trace of his presence. One day, God willing, when things got better, he'd pay it all back with interest. Churches were supposed to be about helping the poor and welcoming the stranger, weren't they?

He pulled the sleeping bag and tightly rolled yoga mat out of his backpack and spread them out on the hard-packed dirt floor. If he made it through this first night without being discovered, he would do it again tomorrow. After night three with no mishaps, he'd take the church key and have a copy made for himself. Then he could set up housekeeping. He took one last look around, curled into his sleeping bag, wiggled himself into a comfortable position, and slept like a rock.

On The first Wednesday in September, her first official day as Interim Minister at First Parish Church in Loring by the Sea, Franklin Bowen, President of the Board of the local historical society and self-appointed defender of the churchly realm, offered to give Olympia Brown a tour of the building. It was clear from the moment he introduced himself that he took great pride in this church. He was proud of the place it held in the social and religious history of the village. He was proud of the clean, simple lines of its classic New England architecture, and he made clear to Olympia that he was determined to see every bit of it preserved at all costs.

"Some things weren't meant to change," he said with more emphasis than might have been necessary. "And this building and its rightful place in history are two of them."

When the two were inside the church proper, he stood at the foot of the high pulpit and swung his arm in a wide arc.

"This, right here, is the original structure. Goes all the way back to the mid seventeen hundreds. Not much is left, of course, but we kept as much of the original building intact as we could when we started adding on. The high pulpit and the first ten rows in the center, five on each side, that's all there was back then. We still have some of those original box pews on display in the parish hall. Can't say they're very comfortable though." He chuckled. "I'm not all that well padded, myself."

Olympia thought of her own built-in insulation and said nothing as Franklin warmed to a story he'd told many times.

"We got the new ones in eighteen-fifties. Then, after the First World War, the Alliance Ladies made the seat cushions. Things don't move too quickly here." It was clear he took pride in that as well.

Olympia nodded. The tour was going on for far longer than she'd anticipated, but it was interesting, and through it, she was getting a sense of what these people valued. The building and its history were at the top of the list. She wondered privately where mission, vision, outreach…and God were positioned on that continuum of ownership—before or after the potlucks and the annual church fair or closeted away with the permanent endowment? All will be revealed, she told herself, and smiled again at Franklin Bowen.

"Now, take a good look at the balcony." He swung his arm in an even broader arc.

Olympia did as she was told.

"We don't use it much anymore. Not so many people in the congregation now. But in the eighteen hundreds, that's where the colored people sat. Now, it's mostly storage."

Then, in quick response to Olympia's look of dismay, he added, "We were the only abolitionists around here back then. Even had a hiding place for runaway slaves in the original cellar. It's all boarded up now, but it's still there. It's not like we weren't already a free state back then, but some churches wouldn't even let the colored step inside the door. 'Course that's all changed now."

Has it really changed that much? thought Olympia. Listening to him, she wasn't so sure.

"Do you have many black families in the congregation?"

He shook his head. "Most of 'em can't afford the real estate around here. Come to think of it, we did have one family some years back, but they moved after the kids graduated from high school. We even bussed some of those METCO kids to schools here in Loring during the seventies. It was a program for poor colored families in the city. We showed them what they could do with themselves if they worked hard." He smiled.

"I see."

If the man was expecting more from the interim minister, he wasn't going to get it, at least not at the moment. This man would take some getting to know.

"Thank you so much, Franklin. You've been very kind to take the time. It's a lot to absorb in one afternoon, but I look forward to learning even more. I really like poking around in lovely old buildings. I like to think about the people who have lived their lives and told their stories inside these walls: people who have been married here, women who had babies who were baptized and sometimes buried on the same day, soldiers who went off to war and never returned. It's a lovely church, and I am really looking forward to being here with you all."

"We have our little ways, Reverend Brown, but we're good people at heart. You just need to get to know us."

"I couldn't agree with you more," she said with a curious smile. That really is the key to so much, isn't?

It was his turn to look perplexed.

She continued. "Building a worthwhile relationship between, say, a minister and a congregation, a husband and wife or any more recent variation thereof, going from stranger to friend, is about taking the time necessary to get past first impressions and assumed expectations. Wouldn't you say that, Mr. Bowen?"

He folded his arms and arched one eyebrow. "You know, I

hadn't really thought about it in those particular terms, but you certainly have given me some food for thought."

"Eat hearty," she thought, and keeping that particular snarky retort to herself, she said aloud, "All in a day's work, Mr. Bowen…at least in my work, anyway."

"Oh, do please call me Franklin."

"Of course. I will indeed."

EMILIO VIEIRA ENTERED the church for the first time on a brisk Sunday morning in late October. He slipped into the back row a few minutes after the service had begun and then just as quietly slipped back out just before the last verse of the final hymn. Only Olympia had seen him come and go because she was the only one facing the rear of the church. She briefly wondered who it might be. It was not uncommon for newcomers or prospective members to check out a new church for weeks without ever speaking to anyone. She referred to it as casing the joint but never where anyone could hear her. Church shopping was the more commonly accepted term. When she looked up a second time, he was gone. She raised her hands in benediction and concluded the service.

EMILIO'S second visit to the upstairs parts of the church was a few days later, in early November, when the Alliance Ladies were having a pre-Thanksgiving bake sale.

"Buy it and eat it right here," they encouraged all who entered. "And while you're at it, go right ahead and order your holiday pies now, and pick them up later." He took advantage of the invitation and the happy chaos to purchase an enormous molasses raisin cookie. Confection in hand, he casually reviewed the layout of the building.

The parish hall, where the sale was in full swing, had been erected next to the much older historic part of the church in the 1950s. The two had remained separate buildings for almost fifty years. Then at the turn of the present century, a large bequest allowed them to create a connecting structure with space for church offices and a long hallway that permitted the members a dry passage from the sanctuary to the social hall and toilets on a Sunday morning. Progress!

He looked around. Still holding his half-eaten cookie, he slipped away from cheerful chatter of the bake sale, quietly let himself into the sanctuary, and sat down in one of the pews so he could more fully acquaint himself with the space. It was pretty much what he expected from his careful reading of the old maps and plans he'd worked through over the months.

Having been raised a Catholic in his native Brazil, Emilio was familiar with ornate and highly embellished church interiors. He was not used to the traditional, stark, white-walled simplicity of a New England meeting house. But within a few minutes, he found it curiously pleasant. He wondered if God could ever be present and happy without a riot of color on the walls and ceilings, without the musty smell of incense and candles in the air, and without the smoky faces of wooden and plaster saints watching from alcoves and peering out from behind the dark and threatening confessionals.

He didn't spend a lot of time thinking about God these days. He didn't spend a lot of time doing anything other than earning money to send to his family in Brazil. Like so many others, Emilio lived and worked in the shadows of the American Dream. But unlike many of the others who lived under the radar, Emilio was educated. He could read and write fluently in English, but his spoken English was still heavily accented. He held a master's degree in economics and had taught the subject in a small college before coming to the States on a study-research visa.

Now, with the visa expired, he washed dishes in a high-end seaside restaurant in Loring by the Sea, and on a good day, if they were really busy, they handed him a uniform and allowed him to wait on tables. Waiting tables made it a really good day. The money was good. The life he lived was not. He was Emilio, a man with no last name, who lived in the shadows and got around on a good, sturdy bicycle he'd found at the dump and fixed up—a man who, now that the weather was turning cold, decided it might be a good idea if he started going to church.

Reverend Olympia Brown had been the interim minister at First Parish Loring by the Sea for almost two and a half months the night Emilio Vieira unlocked the door with his own key and moved into the secret closet under the forgotten stairway. A bleak New England November had settled over land and sea, and people were hunkering down. The clocks had been set back, and the days were getting shorter and relentlessly colder. The skunks and raccoons had already retired to their dens. The squirrels, who didn't hibernate, were still frantically stashing acorns for the months ahead, but the gleanings were sparse. The shortness of day and the length of night made it easier for Emilio to get around town on his bike without attracting too much notice, but the cold made it hard going. And now, with an underground den of his own, not unlike those of the skunks and the raccoons, he would be safe and warm for the winter. He'd planned it all out so very carefully, and *obrigado a Deus*—thank you, God—it was working.

Things didn't always go well for Emilio, but that night he dared to allow himself to think that maybe his luck was about to change. He always waited until well after dark to enter the building, and then using his cell phone as an alarm, he was up and out before first light and on his way to a nearby twenty-four-hour McDonald's or Dunkin' Donuts.

No one in the congregation had the faintest idea that a stranger had taken up residence underneath their comfortably well-shod feet. Upstairs in the historic building, church life went on without interruption, and congregational wheels turned according to their long established traditions. Olympia worked on both of these, the congregational straitjackets of tradition and predictability, but not so obviously that anyone complained. Not yet, anyway. There was a time for everything.

She loved the rhythms of the church year and the cycle of the seasons. She loved how they intersected and contributed to the character and the souls of these hardy, irascible New Englanders. She found the changes of light and temperature energizing and exhilarating. The gathering in and settling down in the fall was comforting, and the New England storms, blizzards and savage nor'easters were terrifyingly beautiful. They were the stuff of prayers and poems, and any number of sermons. This was her world.

The job of an interim minister was to take a congregation through the transition from their previous pastor into the search for a new minister. If, while she was there, she could help them look beyond their own noses, to look outward instead of inward, it would be an added bonus.

"Make haste slowly," her mother always told her. This was one of her mother's oft-repeated admonitions she'd learned by heart.

By early December, she knew all of her parishioners by name. She listened to their stories, told some of her own, and developed a genuine fondness for them all. Of course, as in any line of work, some people were easier to love than others, but that came with the territory. Her job was to serve them all and guide them through the process that would eventually lead to the selection of their new minister.

However, if she were to be really honest with herself, it would also be to help guide this particular community to a place and a vision that went beyond the walls of the building and its glorified past. This, she wisely kept to herself. Food for thought maybe, but not yet ready for prime time.

When she'd accepted the position, they assured her that theirs was a small, somewhat conservative, but very loyal congregation. They were proud of their long colonial history and proud of their fierce independence. They insisted they had few real problems, aside from the usual ones of having an aging congregation, an aging building, and too few people doing most of the work. They were a caring community, they told her. They were people who looked after one another, helped out when needed, and when not needed, they minded their own business. Olympia had heard all of this before but graciously kept it to herself.

And so it was, alone in her office on a Tuesday morning in early December, Olympia leaned on her elbows, stared at her calendar, and thought about the upcoming week. Meetings, home and hospital visits, plans for the Christmas Eve service, and that Sunday's sermon all needed to be considered and scheduled in.

Totally absorbed in her thinking, she was startled by the sharp *snap-click* of the outside door opening. A quick glance at her calendar indicated nothing was scheduled. But in this church, it was not uncommon for people to drop in unannounced and carrying two cups of coffee if they saw her car in the lot and a light in the office. People didn't lock their doors in this town. Life here was more casual.

She heard whispered words and the sounds of footsteps

approaching the office. She looked up to see a tall, attractive woman wearing a knitted cap pulled well down over her dark-brown hair, holding the hands of two little red-haired girls. Olympia had never seen them before. A new young family? Someone church shopping? Someone asking directions or needing to use the bathroom? None of the above? Olympia stood and smiled in welcome, but in the instant their eyes met, she saw a troubled and fearful woman.

"Are you Reverend Brown?"

Olympia waved them in.

"I am indeed. Come in and sit down. Would you like some coffee or juice for the girls? Water? Let's get you all comfortable first. Then you can tell me what brings you here on this chilly-willy morning."

The automatic offer of hospitality served two purposes. It was a gesture of welcome, but it was also a bit of silliness that worked to ease the tension of the unfamiliar and bring a cautious smile to the faces of the two big-eyed children.

The woman stepped into the warmth of the comfortable office but stopped and remained just inside the door.

"Uh, no coffee or juice, thanks. Maybe later. You don't know me...but...well, I need some help with a...personal situation, and I didn't exactly know who to turn to or where to go. I'm not a member here, but we live in town. I've been planning to come in and check it out for some time. I wanted a place to bring the girls. I think children need some sort of religious foundation, don't you?"

The woman stopped, as if uncertain as to what to say next. Olympia waited as she glanced toward the door as though she wanted to turn tail and bolt, but after a moment, she looked back at Olympia stayed her ground.

"Well, being a minister, of course I'm going to say yes, but it's usually more than religion that brings people to church. It's also about community and a sense of belonging. I'm getting ahead of myself. Do sit down, and let's start with your name and the names of these lovely little people you brought with you. Are they twins?"

The woman nodded. "My name is Andrea, Andrea Riggs. These are my daughters, Julianne and Marybeth. And yes, they're twins…fraternal twins. They're six and a half years old."

"I'm the oldest." Julianne stood up a little straighter.

"Okay, Andrea and Julianne and Marybeth, why don't you take off your hats and jackets? There are a couple of low hooks on the back of the door. You can hang them up there and then sit anywhere you want."

Andrea, with her two daughters close beside her, took up residence on the edge of the loveseat opposite Olympia's desk. Olympia pulled up a chair and sat facing them over a sturdy, well-used coffee table. She noticed that Andrea was still wearing her knitted cap but said nothing.

Olympia leaned down and pulled out the toy basket she kept stashed under the table for such occasions. "Would you two like to see what you can find in here to play with while your mother and I visit? I know there's some paper and some crayons in there because I put them in there myself."

The twins looked up at their mother, and with her nod of approval, they slid off the couch and reached for the basket Olympia held out to them.

"If you'd like to sit at my desk and color, I'll get another chair and drag it over so you can sit together. How about that?"

The eager kids were already on their way as Olympia pulled a second chair into place. But before returning to her own chair, she turned on the little radio she kept on the bookcase beside her desk. An NPR music and talk program would act as a sound curtain and provide her and Andrea with at least a modicum of privacy. Within minutes, the girls were coloring, chatting back and forth, and oblivious to anything beyond the crayons, the paper, and each other. The diversion and resettling of the children also gave their mother a chance to compose herself and gather her own thoughts.

4

Olympia fussed with the radio for a bit longer before returning to her seat. "Now then, Andrea, I think we might have a few minutes to ourselves. Tell me, how I can help you?"

In a quick motion, Andrea turned her head to one side and lifted the knitted cap off her head to uncover a raw and ragged bald patch. Olympia gasped and clapped her hand over her mouth.

Just as quickly, Andrea pulled it back on and spoke in a harsh whisper. "I don't want the girls to see it. I've just left the man who did this to me, and I have no place to go. He's a doctor, and he works in downtown Boston. He'll be out of the house until late tonight, so I've got some time before he finds out." She pushed away a strand of hair. "I know it's asking a lot, but is there any way you might help me find a place to stay for a few days so I can think about what to do next? I've lived here in Loring for several years now, but I really don't know anything about the area... I didn't go out very much."

The distraught woman covered her face with her hands and took a deep breath before looking up at Olympia. "This kind of thing happens to other people, not me. I'm a doctor myself, for God's sake. I'm supposed to be better than this. My husband wanted me to take some time to be at home when the twins were born. It didn't seem unreasonable at first, but it was straight downhill from there. In six years, I've gone from being a respected physician in my own right to a cowering slave afraid of my own shadow, afraid of doing anything that would set him off." She paused again. "And everything sets him off. There was no escape, and it kept getting worse….." She pointed to her head. "Then this happened, and I knew that if I didn't get out of there, he'd kill me the next time. So here I am, Reverend. I'm running for my life, and I don't know where to go."

Despite her efforts to blink them back, her light-brown eyes overflowed, and two renegade tears made their way down her cheeks to her trembling chin. She wiped them away and continued in a low whisper. "The girls don't know this is permanent. I have no idea how much they know about what was going on."

They probably know one hell of a lot more than you suspect, thought Olympia.

Andrea shook her head. "This morning`, I told them that instead of going to school, we were going on a mystery trip. I said it was going to be our special secret, and if they told anyone, it wouldn't be a surprise anymore, and the magic would disappear. They think it's a game." More tears and another impatient swipe with the back of her hand. "After my husband left for work and before they got up, I packed up as much as I could and stuffed it in the trunk of the car so they wouldn't see the boxes. He leaves at six on the dot every morning, so I knew I had some time. When they got up, I tried to keep things as routine as possible and said nothing until we were ready to leave. Before we left, I told them to take some of their favorite toys to play with in the car."

She shook her head and sniffled. "And here I am. The great escape. I made it all the way to the center of town.

Three blocks from the house. Some getaway! He always told me I could screw up a free lunch. Maybe he is right. I am a total loser." She paused. "I didn't use to be this way."

Olympia held out a second tissue. "I think you've come to exactly the right place. Churches are supposed to be sanctuaries, are they not? Depending on exactly what you are looking for, I think I might have an idea—at least for the short term."

Andrea took the tissue, wiped her eyes, and blew her nose.

"You okay, Mummy?" It was Julianne.

"My nose decided to run, honey. I might have to ask you to go catch it for me."

Julianne laughed, and Olympia got out of her chair and went back to her desk. "I have a couple of packets of pretzels if you'd like a little something to munch on while you're coloring. May I give them some, Andrea?"

The mother nodded. "They'll want a drink next."

"Already thought of that." Olympia opened a cupboard and pulled out four bottles of water. One for everyone.

"You know one of these is going to get spilled."

"I thought of that too. Water happens! I have a roll of paper towels in the bottom drawer." Olympia chuckled. "Been there, done that. I raised two boys. We spilled a lot of things. Now, where were we?"

"You said you had an idea."

"I do, but I need to ask you a few things first."

Andrea tipped her head to one side and winced. "My scalp hurts."

"You need medical attention."

"I'll tend to it later...I'm a doctor, remember." A sad smile. "Lot of good it did me."

"Do you know if you want to stay in the vicinity or get as far away as possible?" Olympia hesitated. "Hold on, I guess the first question is, do you need money?"

"I'm okay for now. I cleaned out the housekeeping account on the way over here, and I have an IRA left over

from when I was working. I never told my husband about it."
Andrea held up her index finger. "Score one for me. It's there
if I need it. I could go to a hotel somewhere down on the
Cape for a while, but then what? There's no way I'm going to
a canvas cot in a shelter or a welfare motel."

"Do you have family you can go and stay with? Any
friends who could help you?"

Andrea shook her head. "Not an option. My family tried
to discourage me from marrying him. I'm not going to give
them the satisfaction of crawling back in disgrace. Besides,
they're in Nebraska. And I don't have any close friends. Not
now, anyway. He took care of that long ago. I know him. The
first place he'd go looking would be my family, and after that,
he'd go after my friends. I can't involve them—at least not yet.
James, my husband, is a brilliant and successful cardiologist,
but he's also a vicious control freak. You'd never know it to
talk to him, but he's two different people. There's the professional person, the clever gifted doctor, and the private one…"
She glanced over at her children. "…which was something
else."

As a mother of once-young children, Olympia knew the
twins were not going to stay occupied much longer, and she
had no idea how this next few minutes would go. But in her
heart, she knew it was the only thing she could do. She
offered Andrea another tissue.

"I said I had an idea, and before you say yea or nay, just
hear me out. I live about twenty miles from here in a huge old
house with my quirky English husband and two cats. I understand that you've just met me, you are severely traumatized
and in physical pain, and I am asking you to trust me. I'm
suggesting… no, I'm inviting you and the girls to come and
stay with us until you get yourselves sorted out. That could be
a night, or a week or a month. It's a big old farmhouse, and
you and the girls would have your own rooms. It would be a
safe place for you all to stay until you can think this through

more fully. I agree with you. You absolutely don't belong alone in a motel or in a homeless shelter."

Andrea stiffened, and her eyes grew wide and dark. "If by that you mean until I come to my senses and go back, the answer is no."

Now it was Olympia's turn to hold up her hand. "Hold on. I never said that, and I didn't intend to imply it. I'm a minister, and I do believe in the sanctity of marriage, when it is working for both individuals. I do not believe in the practices of human bondage, exploitation, or cruelty or in the domination of one human being over another. You won't be the first woman I've taken into my home." Olympia bit her lip. "And sadly, I'm afraid you won't be the last."

"I'm sorry," whispered Andrea. "I'm terrified, and my scalp still feels like it's on fire. To be honest, I'm afraid for my life. James told me if I ever said one word against him in public or did anything to threaten his career or tarnish his reputation, he'd kill me." She paused. "He's a man of his word, Reverend. He doesn't get mad; he gets even."

She was beyond tears now—a frightened animal fighting for her life and the safety of her cubs.

Olympia held out a gentle, calming hand, and after a moment's hesitation, Andrea placed her own hand in it and looked directly into the minister's eyes. "Thank you, Reverend. And I don't know why I'm doing this, but yes, I accept. Thank you."

"Mummy, I have to go to the bathroom."

"Me too."

"When are we going on our mystery trip?"

"How are we going to do it?"

"Are there clues? Do we have a map?"

"Do we get a prize?"

Andrea looked past Olympia and at the two girls. "Let's start with the bathroom, and then I think the reverend might have the first clue."

Olympia stood and walked Andrea and the girls into the outer office. By then, Gordon Bennett, the church administrator, had come in and sat at his desk sorting the mail.

"Oh, hi, Gordy. I didn't hear you come in. Have you been here long? This is Andrea Riggs and her two daughters, Julianne and Marybeth."

He nodded a quick greeting as she whisked them past and pointed to the bathroom.

"Your door was closed, and I heard voices. That meant you were busy. I didn't need to announce my arrival, so I sat down and got myself to work." He nodded toward the corridor. "I've not seen them before. New parishioners? Somebody church shopping?"

"Yes and no. Look, when they come back, can you keep them busy out here for a few minutes? Maybe ask them if they'd like to see the sanctuary or take a look at the children's area. I need to make a couple of quick phone calls."

"Sure thing, Reverend, anything else?"

"I don't think so, at least not now, anyway. Thanks, Gordy. Special handling on this one. Okay? Details to follow when I can."

Gordy loved being on the inside of anything. He'd been with the church for years, and like so many of them, felt a personal loyalty to and pride in the church and its people. He responded with a wink and a thumbs-up and returned to his work.

5

Back in her office with the door closed, Olympia dialed Frederick's cell phone number. He would be at the bookstore. As a rule, she didn't call him at work, but this was an emergency. She listened to the dialing bleeps and waited, tapping her fingers on the still-open calendar in front of her. He picked up on the first ring.

"Good morning, my love. This is an unexpected surprise. To what do I owe the pleasure of this call?"

Skipping over their usual playful banter, Olympia got straight to the point. "Good morning yourself. I've got an emergency here at the church. A mother and her six-year-old twin daughters just walked into my office, and they're in need of temporary shelter from an abusive situation. I've asked them to come and stay with us in Brookfields until I can get them sorted out and find more permanent safe housing."

"Well, of course. We've got the room. When will they be coming?"

Olympia paused for a nanosecond. "Uh…today….actually. Most likely within the hour. I'm going to leave work and bring them down there myself."

"No car?"

"Sorry, love, that was unclear. They have a car and will follow me to the house. I'll settle them in. The guest rooms are made up and relatively presentable."

"Anything I can do before that?"

"No, just be your wonderful welcoming self when you come home. You're going to love the kids. They're really cute. The poor mother is kind of in shock, but she's thinking fairly clearly. It shouldn't be for too long. We'll just need a couple of days to come up with a plan. It's a complicated situation."

"Should I call Father Jim? I seem to remember, he found you a safe house for another abused woman."

Olympia smiled at the phone. This was so typical of Frederick. When it came to helping someone, say yes first, ask questions later.

"Not yet, but I suspect I'll be needing his advice eventually. We have to get the mother and kids safe and settled in first. What time will you be home this afternoon?"

"Usual time. Around four."

"Good, see you then."

"Jolly good!"

"Frederick?"

"Mmmm?"

"I love you."

"Well that's all right then."

Smiling, Olympia clicked off the phone and went back to the outer office to collect her tattered little family and take them home.

As a precaution against one losing sight of the other and Andrea getting lost, the two women exchanged phone numbers, and Olympia wrote out directions, along with her street address, on the back of an old envelope.

"Covering all the bases," she said with what she hoped was an encouraging smile.

"I'm glad one of us is thinking straight," said Andrea.

"And we both know it's not me. I don't know how to thank you for this, but believe me, I'll find a way....eventually."

Olympia brushed away the thought. "Let's not worry about that right now, okay? And besides, I believe in paying forward. I help you, and you help the next person down the line. Then the good stuff gets spread around instead of getting stuck all in one place."

"Works for me." For the first time that day, Andrea favored Olympia with a fragment of a smile.

"Are we going on our mystery ride now?" asked Julianne.

"Indeed, we are," said Olympia. "And I have an idea. When my boys were little and we were going on a ride, we played the red-car game. Whoever is the first to see a red car along the way gets to keep it. The person with the most cars when you get there wins."

"What do you win?" Marybeth asked.

"When my kids played, the winner didn't have to do the dishes that night. I suppose we'll have to come up with something else for you two."

"I know," said Julianne. "How about the winner doesn't have to eat her vegetables?"

"I'm sure we'll think of something," said Olympia.

The two women made it back to Brookfield without incident and with only two or three "Are we there yets?" in the Riggs minivan. A badly calculated red light separated the two vehicles for a couple of blocks, but they soon reconnected. When the two cars pulled into the gravel drive and parked behind the back of the house, totally out of view from the street, it was almost 1:00 p.m.

Lunch would be the first order of the day. Everything is easier with a full tummy. Any mother knows that. Olympia kept peanut butter and jelly, tuna fish, canned soup, and saltines on hand at all times. Emergency rations. The wine, cheese, and chocolate would come later. Didn't it say somewhere in the Bible there was a time and a season for everything under heaven—even, and sometimes, especially, chocolate? Olympia smiled at her own irreverence and reached into the cupboard for the peanut butter.

As WINTER APPROACHED, Emilio asked the manager for double shifts at the restaurant whenever he could. It was as much for keeping busy and out of the cold as it was for the money. In the warm days of summer, there were any number of places Emilio could go to keep himself occupied. But with the cold weather upon them, his options were considerably reduced. Movies cost money, even matinees. He made regular visits to the library where he could read, study, use the computer, and stay warm. He was a familiar face in the local coffee shops, but he didn't want to become too familiar a face anywhere. As an immigrant without documentation, he could be an easy target for anyone in white, suburban Loring by the Sea with a grudge against brown-skinned people who spoke accented English.

Emilio remained unobtrusively on the edges and on the move. He was always pleasant and agreeable whenever he did have a casual conversation, but took care never to reveal anything personal. Then he would move away as soon as he could without appearing rude or hostile.

Even when he attended the Sunday services upstairs in the church—one more way to keep warm—he remained courteously and carefully apart. He spoke easily when spoken to, made light conversation when required, and even helped with moving chairs and tables for the coffee hour after church. People knew him by his name only, Emilio, or as that nice Brazilian boy who always sat at the back of the church. It worked for them, and it worked for him.

By now, he'd pretty much memorized the schedule of the church's comings and goings. No one ever got in there before nine in the morning, so he made sure he was up and out by eight at the very latest. Most evenings, even if there was a Ladies Alliance meeting or an AA meeting, the place was never active later than ten during the week and only occasionally a little later on the weekend. He'd learned to wait and watch until he was sure it was safe to enter. Then he'd hide his bike in the thick tangle of untended bushes behind the church and let himself in. Once inside, having long since memorized every step of the way, he'd make his way down to his nest and only turn on a light when he'd pulled the creaky wooden door tightly shut behind him. Shortly after he moved in, he found some rags and blocked the lone grimy window on the far wall so that no one from outside would ever notice light or movement and suspect there was anything inside… beyond dust and rags.

Emilio did not see himself as squatting or taking advantage of something that wasn't his. He saw it as making use of an empty space. If his spoken English were more fluent, he'd say he was repurposing it. He used very little electricity—only enough to power an LED camping lantern he'd found at the church rummage sale—and a little bit more to charge up his phone. The furnace provided enough heat to keep him from freezing, and he supplemented this with a yard-sale sleeping bag and a Salvation Army store woolen army blanket. More recently, he'd pulled a low, folding beach chair out of a dumpster and found a couple of plastic milk crates that served as both a table and as storage. He used the church bathrooms for personal needs and occasionally heated something up in the spacious kitchen, careful never to leave any trace of his being there. If a toilet flushed in the middle of the night or a microwave dinged and nobody heard it, did it really happen?

That particular night, Emilio was tired and desperately wanted to get in out of the cold, but the choir was still rehearsing the music for the Christmas Eve service. At one point, he actually thought about joining the choir as a way to keep out of the weather, but that would cause these friendly people to ask more questions. So he stood in the dark, holding on to his bike, shivering and listening to the words of "O Come all Ye Faithful" leaking out through the church windows.

He was used to warm and sunny Christmases back in Brazil. This would be his first cold, dark, and lonely Christmas away from home. He shivered. Still, the thought that he was providing for the safety and well-being of his family made up for the discomfort. Someday, he would bring them here to the land of opportunity. Maybe not to Loring by the Sea. He wouldn't be making that kind of money—but here, to America, the land of opportunity.

One day, he would have a place with more than one room and with space for a garden in the back. He shivered again, but imagined he felt better, warmed by his own thoughts and the sight of the choir members straggling out of the church. They talked and laughed amongst themselves, some even singing a few lines of the hymns into the night air. Going home. One day, he thought. One day I'll have a home to go to and a car of my own that I can drive to get myself anywhere I want. He sneezed.

SHORTLY AFTER LUNCH on that same day, Dr. James Cabot called home to tell his wife he was going to stay the night in Boston. When she didn't pick up the house phone, he left a terse message and tried her cell phone only to have it switch him immediately to voice mail. Flushed with irritation and with no other alternative, he thumped out a five-word text message. "Where the hell are you?" He hit send and then immediately bashed out another. "I'm coming home. I'm coming home now. You'd better fucking be there."

He made a second call, this one to courteously and

graciously confirm his plans for dinner that evening, and to say that, if the invitation were still open, he would be spending the night.

"I might be a few minutes late," he said smoothly with no trace of irritation or tension in his voice. "Something's come up that needs my attention, but it shouldn't delay me for very long."

Cabot took perverse and sadistic pleasure in unsettling his wife. He had no intention of going home.

6

Standing in Olympia's pleasantly cluttered kitchen, Andrea Riggs pulled her phone out her pocket, saying she needed to check her messages.

With a look of alarm on her face, Olympia held up her hand and yelled, "Wait! Don't turn it on."

"I'll only be a minute. Nobody ever calls me."

"No, I mean it. Don't turn it on. A cell phone can act as a GPS locator. If you turn that thing on, your husband, if he is tech savvy at all, will know exactly where you are. You need to get rid of it or at least put it away and get a disposable one. Meanwhile, for God's sake, don't use it."

"Oh, my God, I never thought... I mean, I knew about that, but right now... Well, I'm not thinking very clearly."

"You're doing fine, Andrea. Why don't you get the kids settled upstairs in their room, and then I can run a couple of ideas by you."

She cocked her head to one side and raised her eyebrows. She still wore the knitted cap.

"A couple of ideas? More than one. You don't waste any time, do you?"

Olympia smiled and nodded. "I know of a safe place. It's

less than a half hour from here. If it's available, I think you and the girls can probably stay there for as long as you need to."

"Where?"

"It's one town south of here, in Plymouth. A friend of mine owns it. We've recently done some work together. She's safe and savvy, but I think it's better if you get the girls into bed before we talk about it. We have time, and as long as you keep your phone off, there's no way in hell your husband can track you down. He's not likely to go to the police, is he?"

She shook her head. "That's the last thing he'd do. He's a law unto himself, Reverend, and he writes all the rules. Asking for help is admitting weakness." She shook her head and winced. "Never going to happen. He might hire a private detective if it comes to it, but no one would ever know. It's all about image with him." Again, she shook her head and chewed on her lower lip. "If they only knew."

With that, Andrea gathered up her girls and started them up the stairs for baths and bed.

"So is this the mystery place?" asked Marybeth. "Are we here?"

"When are we going home?" asked Julianne.

"How about you each get to ask one question when you are all tucked in?"

"Me first," said Julianne.

"Aww, you always go first," complained Marybeth.

"I'll pick a number," said their weary mother. "And the one who guesses it, goes first."

It was almost an hour before Andrea, now clearly exhausted from the day and the bathing and bedding down of the children, returned to the living room where Olympia sat knitting and Frederick worked a crossword over and around a cat that was firmly anchored in his lap.

"Whew, I didn't think they'd ever settle down."

"Not surprising," said Olympia with a look of compassion

and understanding. "Different place, different beds, different routine, a distracted mom doing her best not to let it show. They'll probably be up before the sun tomorrow as well. It'll take a few days for them to settle in."

"I hope we'll have moved on by then, Reverend. I don't want to be an intrusion or a burden."

Olympia shook her head. "You are neither an intrusion nor a burden—or anything else for that matter. We have a huge house with bedrooms and cats to spare. I already told you, this isn't the first time we've had someone come stay with us who needed some time to think, and I know damn sure it won't be the last."

Andrea laughed out loud, and the unspoken tension in the room began to subside. She turned toward Olympia with a questioning look.

"While you were upstairs, I called that friend of mine in Plymouth, the one with the B and B...."

Andrea blinked and interrupted Olympia. "Um, excuse me, but that might be too expensive. I mean, I'm not looking a gift horse in the mouth or anything, but those places can run two and three hundred dollars a night. I couldn't manage that over the long term." She took a shaky breath.

"Nothing of the sort, Andrea. She runs a legitimate B and B for the rich people, and for a couple of years now, she's kept an unregistered apartment downstairs in the main house for people in need, particularly for women and children escaping abuse. It's a sweet little place, two bedrooms, kitchenette, table and chairs, and a sitting room. All that and an ocean view. It's got everything you'll need, even linens and a TV. There's private parking and a private entrance around the back where no one would ever see you coming or going, and the best part is, there's no charge."

By now, Andrea had gone completely wide-eyed while Frederick stroked the cat curled in his lap. He knew what was coming next. He'd had the good fortune to meet the kindly mystery lady earlier in the year, and he knew of her quiet, good works… and her colorful past.

"Anyway," continued Olympia. "When you were upstairs, I called her. She said the place would be available in a week or so and that you were more than welcome to come and stay for as long as you needed. She told me she'd call me the minute it was available. You are going to absolutely love that woman. She really is something else."

From where she was sitting, Andrea couldn't see Frederick roll his eyes. And for the time being, anyway, it was probably just as well. Everything in due time, thought Olympia.

WRAPPED in multiple layers and hidden away in his underground nest, Emilio sneezed several more times. He knew by then he was coming down with a cold. This was not good, but he'd had colds before and knew they would eventually go away. Drink lots of water, get some vitamin C at the drugstore, keep warm and rest as much and often as he could.

Unfortunately, with the holidays coming on, the restaurant was crazy busy, and the manager wanted all hands on deck. The tips were good, the hours were as many as he could handle, and of course, he needed the money for his family. Resting was not going to be an option unless he remained secretly holed up in his mini-cave during the day. Other than that, there wasn't any place he could stretch out and rest even if he wanted to. Emilio had worked through colds before. And he could do it again. He pulled the sleeping bag tighter around his shoulders, and when that was not really enough, he reached out one arm and fumbled around in the dark for his wooly cap. *That was the worst thing about colds: they made you cold.* Emilio shivered then remembered seeing blankets in the children's room. If, in an hour he was awake and still cold, he'd crawl out there and find himself another one. He burrowed deeper into his wrappings and let the memory of the sunny warmth of December in his native country and the familiar sounds and smells of his neighborhood comfort him and carry him into sleep.

AT MIDNIGHT, well past her usual bedtime, Olympia was still wide awake and feeling restless. Andrea, her two daughters, and Frederick were all in bed. The house was quiet and quickly cooling down on the December night. Even the two cats had abandoned her in favor of curling up against Frederick in the marital bed. She considered poking one more log into the wood stove, but instead, pulled up an afghan knitted years ago by her mother. Comforted, she reached out for the hand-bound leather diary she kept beside her chair. She'd come upon the diary shortly after moving into the rambling old New England farmhouse that was now her home. The diary and an old wooden beehive clock that only worked when it had something to say had both belonged to the last Mayflower Winslow descendent to live in the house. The author of this precious volume was a strong, proud, independent woman, ahead of her time, named Leanna Faith Winslow.

Over the years of living in the house and reading the diary, Olympia had developed a strong feeling of kinship with the author, a woman who, she learned, possessed many of her own characteristics and personality traits. Or was it the other way around? As she read and sometimes reread the contents of the diary, Olympia felt as though she knew Leanna Faith intimately and often turned to her private writings when she felt she needed advice or guidance.

And then there was the matter of the clock—the clock that didn't work unless it had something to say. It had been a while before she and Frederick realized that the clock, although it never did tell the time of day, had plenty of other things to tell them. Through a series of *bings* and *bongs* and a few more untimely actions, the opinionated clock monitored their activities, offered unsolicited advice, and looked after their safety. Two or more clangs for impending trouble…or on good days, when the domestic waters were calm and things were going smoothly, they were sometimes rewarded with a single musical *bing* of affirmation.

As if on cue, when Olympia lifted and opened the diary, the clock favored her with a gentle *bing*.

"I'll take that as a yes." Olympia nodded in the direction of the clock.

November, 1865

Why is it that seasons seem to come and go more quickly now? My beloved Aunt Louisa often asked that question in her later years. Was it not only yesterday that Susan and I were complaining about the oppressive heat? And now, in what feels like the blink of an eye, the trees are bare, and I have already seen a few tentative flakes of snow. Nothing of any measure as yet, although I must say that my Jonathan and Susan's daughter Annabelle, inseparable now, look out the window every morning in hopes of finding a white surprise. It won't be long, I tell them, but they are children, and waiting is so very hard.

The dreadful war is over, and Susan's husband has returned from the battlefront. Praise God! For the present, he has joined us, and we four make quite a lovely little family, but it will be some time before he is fit to seek proper employment. His war-wounds are not the kind that can be stitched up or reset like a broken bone. His wounds are of the heart and of the spirit, and as such, will be slow in healing. Susan is overjoyed with his return. I am so grateful to be able to have him stay and mend with us.

And speaking of Susan, I will say in the privacy of these pages, that it has been most agreeable to have a companion of my own age and one who is in possession of similar intellect and interests to my own. We've become quite a formidable pair, we two, speaking up and out in the cause of suffrage for women, and more recently, working in the abolitionist movement with the Quakers here in Cambridge. I understand there is another active Quaker community in New Bedford as well. When I am back in Brookfields for Christmas, perhaps I shall under take to make their acquaintance.

....More anon, LFW

7

The follow morning, Emilio slept though his alarm and woke up feeling groggy, snuffly, and in a panic when he looked at his watch. As it turned out, he didn't need an extra blanket after all, and once he'd fallen sleep, he'd made it all the way through the night. Maybe the cold wouldn't be too bad after all. He tried to look on the bright side whenever he could—anything to keep him going.

Now it was a mad scramble to pull on his clothes and get out of the building before the administrator arrived. He managed to do it, but only just in time. He was pedaling down the street toward the center of town as the first car to arrive at the church turned into the parking lot. The air was damp and chill. He'd read about snow and seen pictures of it but never the real thing. He knew it snowed in Brazil at high altitudes and in the very southern part of the country. But Emilio's family was poor and had no money for luxuries like travel or vacations.

Today, he would bike across town to the library where, as soon as it opened, he'd sit down at one of the computers, check his email on something bigger than his phone, and read the paper. He thought about breakfast, but realized he wasn't really hungry. He would grab something later on at the restaurant. What he needed was water. Plenty to drink was what his mother said when he was a child, and thankfully, that was readily available in the library. He'd be okay. Another sneeze.

But as the day wore on, instead of feeling like he was beating it back, Emilio knew the cold was settling in for the long haul. By the time he got to work, he was shivering again, and when he wasn't shivering, he was sweating.

"Hey man, you okay? You don' look too good," said one of his coworkers.

"I got a col' tha's all." And as if to prove it, he sneezed. "They come, they go, I live."

"Well, you look like sheet, and you soun' worse. Don't sneeze on me, okay?"

Emilio tried to grin but failed. "I won'."

"Maybe you go home? I do your work. You sick, you stay home tomorrow."

"I think about it," croaked Emilio.

AT THE WATKINS/BROWN household, three adults and two children were getting to know one another a little better and a little more easily over the breakfast table. Frederick was usually the first one up, and as was his custom, made a pot of tea for himself and set up the coffee maker so that Olympia could simply hit the start button when she came into the kitchen. Usually, he set it for four cups, but not knowing what their adult guest would be wanting, he set it for eight. Then he filled the teapot to the top, added two more tea bags, and covered it with an oft-mended tea cozy knitted by his own mother. He'd carried it here, along with her blessed memory, all the way from England. Before he set it on the teapot, he held it up to his nose and sniffed. His mother had been a chain-smoker, and he swore he could still smell her cigarette smoke in the yarn. He smiled.

The girls, up early, wanted no part of a cooked breakfast, thank you, but contented themselves with cereal and a fresh orange each. The newness and adventure of it all was still exciting, and they chattered on like two happy little chickadees on a frosty morning. Frederick thought back to mornings around a breakfast table back in England with his brother and sisters. He smiled. Same noise level, different setting. Soon, the twins would wander off in search of Sesame Street, and when they did, the grownups could get down to more serious matters. They needed to talk to the children about why they were there and why they would not be going back home.

OLYMPIA HADN'T MENTIONED it to Andrea yet, but there was the complicated issue of Christmas. It was less than three weeks away. Might as well start with the easy one. She refilled her own mug then waved the pot in Andrea's direction. Andrea nodded and held out her own cup. Thus armed, Olympia called the meeting to order.

"I've been thinking…."

"Look out," said Frederick.

"Quiet, you." She turned toward Andrea. "As I said, I've been thinking that with Christmas coming on, it might be nicer for you all to stay here with us for the holiday and then move into the place in Plymouth after the first of the year. I know I'd love it. We haven't had little kids around the house for Christmas in forever. Think about it. That's all I'm asking. It's not like we don't have the room."

Andrea looked at Olympia over her coffee mug and smiled her gratitude. "That's a lifetime away right now. Thank you, but first things first. I need to find a bargain-priced department store somewhere and get some basics. We have our coats and hats and the shoes and the few things I managed to grab and pack before we left, but that's it."

"Get yourself a cheap, throwaway cell phone while you're out," said Olympia. "And later, we can do something about getting you a new credit card. Meanwhile, if you can, use cash. Checks and cards are too easily traced. Don't do anything that will leave a paper trail."

"You think of everything, don't you?"

Olympia nodded. "Not really, but as I said before, you are not the first abused woman I've helped."

Andrea winced and looked away when Olympia said the word abused.

"And now that I think about it, you probably should take my van, just in case your husband has put a call out on your license plate. Can you drive a stick shift?"

Andrea nodded. "What about you? Don't you have to go over to the church today?"

Olympia rolled her eyes. "I can take Frederick's truck." She paused. "Oh, that's right, you haven't seen it yet. Have you? Bright yellow, vintage Ford pickup. A real collector's item and not exactly something you can ignore. That will get the tongues wagging in Loring by the Sea. The minister showing up in a forty-year-old, daffodil-colored pickup." She chuckled. "The thing is… Well, let's just say it has character, and it runs. What else do I need? I never have worried about appearances, and I'm not going to start now, even in that lovely, little, picture-book town. They need to see how the other half lives."

Andrea cocked her head to one side. "Is it really that bad there? I guess I don't know. I've had almost no contact with anyone in town. James chose the town, picked out the house, and wrote the check, cash, without ever asking me. It was all about location, price, and appearance." She gulped then bit her lip. "Now, look at me, homeless in a borrowed bathrobe with a handful of hair missing."

Olympia reached across the table and took Andrea's hand in hers. "You look great. You look strong. You look healthy, and your hair will grow back. I say you look like a woman who's just done something very brave."

"You really think so?" whispered Andrea.

"Absolutely. Why don't you get dressed, and we can talk about a plan of action. If you want, and if they don't mind, you can leave the kids here with us while you go shopping. Frederick isn't working today, and I won't go in until later to make sure they're settled in. I have a light day."

Andrea's voice grew stronger. "Actually, I was going to ask if I could leave the kids here and have you take me to a rental car agency. That way, I won't inconvenience anyone."

Olympia shook her head. "Uh-uh. Too traceable. You have to show your li...." She clapped a hand to her forehead. "Good gravy, what am I thinking? I'll take you to the rental agency all right, and I'll rent the car in my name, and you can drive it. Problem solved! And for God's sake, don't go anywhere near Loring. You don't want to take a chance on anyone recognizing you."

Andrea gave her a thumbs-up and pushed herself back from the table. "Perfect. I'll go throw on some clothes and get going." She paused. "Now that I think about it, once I get the car, I might be a while. By the time I pick up some necessaries, a new phone, and stuff that I haven't thought of yet, it might be well into the afternoon before I get back."

"Take your time, Andrea. The kids will be fine, and even though you're in somewhat of an altered state right now what with everything that's happened to you in the last twenty-four hours, I say there's nothing like a little retail therapy to get a girl back on her feet. Go for it."

Andrea paused in the doorway and worked up a smile. "Thank you sounds so stupid with all you've done for us, but right now, I don't have any better word for it. So thank you, and if you're sure we won't be a bother, I think I'd like to say yes to Christmas. I may be brave, but I'm not ready to face a family holiday alone."

"I can't think of anything that would be nicer for us, Andrea."

Frederick, who had been sitting there listening while the women talked, added, "Jolly good!"

8

———

By two in the afternoon of the following day, when his wife still hadn't responded to any of his messages, James Cabot cancelled his afternoon appointments and headed south to find a silent, empty house. His wife's car wasn't in the drive or the garage, and there were no signs of supper preparation in their state-of-the-art kitchen. He kicked the door shut then spotted the piece of paper folded in half and wedged between the salt and pepper shakers. His first name was hastily written in her messy doctor's handwriting on the outside. He snatched it up, read it, ripped it into pieces, and flung them in the direction of the sink.

He didn't care what the fucking letter said about not coming back, he'd fucking find her. And when he did, he'd drag her back by what was left of that disgusting mousey-fine hair of hers and really beat the shit out of her. God, he hated that hair. Always had. What the hell did he ever see in her, anyway? A quick fuck? He shook his head in disgust. Not quick enough. Not that it did any good. When she insisted on the in-vitro thing, wouldn't you know, she ended up with two for the price of one. Double trouble and a double reminder that he wasn't man enough to do the job himself.

If he was a drinking man, he would have opened a bottle, but James Cabot didn't drink. Instead, he reached into his pocket, pulled out his plastic pillbox, flipped one out, and gulped it down. He took it for chronic back pain, he told himself. Then, gripping the sides of the granite countertop, he waited for the rage to subside and the all-pervading drug-induced warmth and relaxation to lower his blood pressure and stop the shaking. He forced himself to breathe slowly and deeply while he counted the minutes.

There was work to do, and he was going to need a clear head to do it. Notifying the police was out of the question. This was a private matter, and it was going to stay that way. Nor was calling that bunch of disapproving assholes that she called family an option. He snorted at the very thought of them. Wouldn't this just make their day? Well he'd damn well never give them that I-told-you-so satisfaction.

He stamped his way around the kitchen, kicking at things in his way. It was not as though anyone would notice that she was missing. She had no friends. He'd seen to that long ago. He considered taking a second pill but realized he'd not eaten anything since noon. Maybe he should call for take-out? Nah. There had to be something here. It was merely a question of finding it.

Feeling calmer now, he walked over to the fridge and found some cold cuts that would have been there for the girls' lunch. Leftovers were not allowed in his house, so there was no cold chicken or leftover lasagna he might have heated up. He cursed and pulled out the ham and cheese slices and wondered where she kept the bread. Stupid bitch.

As he slammed together a no-frills sandwich, he was already working out a plan. The most important thing would be to maintain the appearance of business as usual—no change. If she didn't come back in a couple of days, he'd hire a private detective and let him do the work. God knew he had enough money. That way, he wouldn't have to interrupt his hospital schedule, and no one would be the wiser.

"Shit!" He spat out the word into the empty kitchen. "Goddammit!"

Another realization. At some point, somebody from the girls' school was going to call and start asking questions. I'll think of something, he thought, taking a vicious bite out of his dry sandwich. Sick grandmother, that's it. Isn't it always a sick grandmother? Problem solved, at least for now. He went over to the sink, filled a glass with water, and downed half of it. The pills always gave him dry mouth; so did a mouthful of sandwich with no mustard, butter, or mayonnaise.

I'll kill her, he thought, chewing with more force than was necessary. This time, I really will, and because I know exactly how to do it, no one will ever find out how she died. Another swallow of water. Things were starting to fall into place. He sat down at the table to finish his sandwich and wondered if there were any cookies in the pantry. Maybe there was some ice cream in the fridge. Sugar…he needed sugar. He turned and started toward the fridge when the back door burst open, and a hooded stranger holding a gun jerked his head to the side and growled a single word, "Outside."

9

Andrea called in to say that things were taking even longer than expected, and if the girls were content, did Olympia mind if she just stayed out and got everything taken care of?

"Take your time," said Olympia. "I've been over to the church and back, and now I'm home and making my pastoral calls from here. The girls and Frederick are building a tent over the kitchen table, and I'm warm and happy in my office with the two cats. The little beasties never were very fond of camping." Olympia chuckled at her own joke. "In other words, there's no rush. Enjoy your free time, and I'll see you when I see you."

"Would you like me to pick us up something for supper?"

"I'd love it. I'm vegetarian but not picky. And as you may have noticed, I am not undernourished."

Now it was Andrea's turn to laugh. It wasn't a big laugh, but it was a beginning. This woman's been through hell, thought Olympia as she hung up the phone. And while she's still got a long way to go and it's likely that the enormity of everything won't really hit her for a little while yet, I do believe she's taken another baby step forward.

By four in the afternoon, Andrea was still out, but she'd called in a second time to say she'd be back within the hour with Thai take-out. Olympia's mouth started watering at the very sound of the word. Thai was one of their favorites. She closed her office door behind her and went back out into the kitchen to put some beer into the fridge and chill some wine.

The aforementioned tent—an old blanket draped over the table and stretched across the backs of two of the chairs—took up much of the floor space. And by the sound of the stifled giggles coming from underneath it, she knew exactly where the girls were.

"Everything okay in there?" She asked.

More giggles. "We made a tent. Do you think we can sleep in it tonight?"

"Ask your mother."

With nothing else she could think of to do in the kitchen, Olympia decided it would be a paper plates on newspaper meal in front of the TV and the fire. Might as well continue the camping theme, she mused and then with a sigh, dropped heavily into her chair. How did I get so tired? she asked herself as she reached for the TV remote. All this search and rescue is hard work. That, or I'm getting old. She leaned back, aimed the remote, clicked on the news, and then sat bolt upright.

BREAKING NEWS, flashed the crawler at the bottom of the television screen. "Prominent Neurosurgeon, Dr. James Cabot, found shot to death outside his home in Loring by the Sea, an exclusive coastal town in Southeastern Massachusetts."

The street reporter stood outside the fluttering yellow tape that surrounded a multi-level, many-windowed, professionally landscaped house and spoke in solemn tones. She spoke of multiple gunshot wounds, investigative teams, and community outrage. The reporter looked sorrowfully into the camera. "Things like this don't happen in towns like Loring by the

Sea, but your evening anchor team is right here on the scene, bringing you the latest updates as we get them. Right now, we can only say that this appears to be a targeted attack, and people in the surrounding area are not at risk. Police are still trying to locate the next of kin and request that if anyone has any information regarding this case that might be of help to the investigation, to please contact the police."

"Frederick." Olympia forced herself to keep her voice strong and even. The last thing she wanted to do right now was to alert the twins. "Can you come in here right now? No, not in five minutes…right now."

Frederick, who did not like to be interrupted and summoned from a project or even a book was more than mildly irritated when he entered the room. "Well then, what is it?"

By way of an answer, Olympia hit Replay on the remote.

"Jesus Christ," said Frederick, a man not given to epithets of such vehemence. "What the hell do we do now?"

"For starters, we turn off the TV and keep it off until Andrea gets home. And after that, my love, I have absolutely no idea."

As it turned out, the two did not have long to wait before they heard the sound of Andrea's rental car crunching up the driveway.

10

A   t the manager's urging, Emilio did finally agree to leave the restaurant and go home. He was now burning hot and not at all sure he could make it back to the church, but he didn't dare ask for a ride and have someone find out where he was living. Before leaving, he gulped down a cup of hot tea and dug a sweater and an extra hat and scarf out of the lost-and-found box before pushing off. The two miles home had never seemed so long, and he was forced to stop several times to rest and catch what remained of his breath before pressing on. His worst fear was not making it back, but that people would still be in the church, and he would have to wait outside in the cold. The first few fluttery flakes of snow began to fall as the church came into view.

Blessedly, the windows were dark and the parking lot was empty. He gasped out a raspy, *"Obrigado Deus."* And now, too tired and sick to marvel at his first ever snow, he dragged his bike into the bushes and stumbled toward the door. Once inside, even though his brain was fuzzy with the fever and he was shaking all over, he had the good sense to take some extra water from the kitchen and grab an armful of blankets from the children's room. The last mile is always the longest, and to

Emilio, the last thirty feet to his secret bunker were the longest he'd ever traversed.

Once inside and under the stairs, he half crawled, half dragged himself to the place where he'd made his bed. With a low groan, still fully dressed, he rolled himself into it. The last thing he did before he let himself go to sleep was to dig in his pocket and pull out the half-eaten dinner roll he'd picked off a returned plate in the restaurant dish-room. He gave it a weak toss off into the corner where the mouse he'd seen for several nights now would be sure to find it.

Outside, Emilio's first snow was getting heavier and beginning to stick to the grassy areas. Before long, the roads would be covered, and Loring by the Sea would look like a Christmas card. But as everyone knows, looks can be deceptive.

OLYMPIA AND FREDERICK did not have long to think about what to say to Andrea. They heard a car door slam, followed by the sound of the kitchen door opening and the happy squeals of Julianne and Marybeth greeting their mother.

The two sprinted into the kitchen as Andrea, her arms full of shopping bags and the take-out containers, squeezed through the back door. The girls jumped up and down and tried to look at the things their mother was unloading onto the blanket-covered table-tent that was currently taking up much of the kitchen.

"Frederick, uh, can you take the girls out into my office and play a computer game with them or something? There are some crayons and markers out there as well. Maybe they could make a picture for their mother."

"Guess what, girls?" said their mother. "It's starting to snow outside. Maybe we'll have a white Christmas. We'll have to check the weather after supper."

It was clear that Andrea had no idea of what had

happened to her husband. The tantalizing smell of their dinner seemed so out of place now, and Olympia wondered if they would even want anything at all once they knew. Olympia chewed on her lower lip and counted the minutes.

Frederick quietly took the girls in hand to go check on the snow. Then he herded them into Olympia's office to make a picture story of what they did that day to show their mother. Once they were safely out of earshot, Olympia suggested to Andrea that they go into the sitting room.

Andrea was instantly on alert. "What's going on? Has something happened?"

"I'm afraid it has, Andrea. By any chance, have you listened to the news on the radio?"

Wide-eyed now and sitting forward in the chair, she shook her head. "No, I didn't know how to turn it on. What happened?"

Olympia directed Andrea to the sofa then sat down next to her. "Andrea, I wish there was an easier way to say this, but I just learned

on the evening news... your husband has been shot. He's dead."

"Oh, my God."

"Mummy, Mummy, you didn't look at the tent. Come on."

"I... uh..."

"Girls," said Olympia in a firm and gentle tone, "your mother and I are having some grown-up time. Do you think you could go back and finish that picture you started with Frederick? I think we'll have more time to look at the tent after supper."

"They sort of escaped on me," said a troubled-looking Frederick. "Sorry about that."

"They're kids. Break out the cookies and milk. Supper's on hold."

"I hope you don't mind?" asked Olympia.

Andrea shook her head, and when the girls were well out of earshot, she said simply, "What do I do now?"

In all of her years of ministry, Olympia had never been in this situation but knew well that, when in the depths of the darkness, there will come a great light. *Have faith, Olympia. Trust your instincts and your experience.* She reached for the woman's hand.

"Let's start with you. What are you feeling right now?"

Andrea thought for a long moment. "I don't know. Um… shock. Fear for the girls…fear of the future…and…God forgive me …blessed relief."

Olympia nodded and waited for more to come, knowing full well it would. She leaned in close and held the woman's hand.

"I was afraid of him, and I hated him…and I guess I hated myself for letting him do this to me. I'm a doctor myself, for God's sake. How could I have been so stupid? It was never good. I knew right after we got married I'd made a mistake, but I was proud, and I tried to make the best of it. It only kept getting worse. It got really bad after the girls were born. I thought having a child would change things, you know, make it better between us. Just the opposite. The twins were a surprise. That's another story. And as much as I don't want to, I suppose I should call the police and let them know where I am."

She paused for breath. "This just happened, right? While I was out shopping? Oh, my God, I could have been back there when…. It could have been me or the girls… Who would…. Uh, shouldn't we put the supper in the oven?"

Olympia knew that scattered and disjointed thinking was commonplace when a person was in emotional shock, so she was not surprised when Andrea shifted from personal reaction to logistics.

"There'll be time for that," said Olympia. "I think we

need to decide what and when you want to tell the girls before we do anything else."

Andrea covered her face with her hands. "Oh, God, I don't know. Not yet. I need to get my own head around it first. Can you help me when I do?"

"Of course. But you should call the police and let them know where you are and find out what happened so you will know what to say and what not to say to the girls. The thing is, we need to keep them away from the TV for a day or two, but what about their tablets?"

"They only read books and play games on their tablets. We've not let them have anything to do with social media. I guess that might be the one thing we agreed on." A sad smile.

Olympia picked up the house phone and held it out to Andrea. "I wrote down the number. You ready?"

"As ready as I'll ever be, I guess."

"Would you like me to step out of the room?"

Andrea waved off the idea. "Anything but. I'm not sure what to say, what to ask, or…." She shook her head and wordlessly stared at the phone in her hand.

"Say, why don't I make the call? I'll tell them who I am and that I have you and the girls safe here with me? Then I can hand over the phone, and you can talk to them."

"Sure." Andrea's voice was flat, and her shoulders slumped, but it was clear from the strength in her voice that she was ready.

"Mummmyyyyyyyyyyyyyyyyyyyyyyy?"

"I'm on the phone, girls. I'll be off in a few minutes. Then we can talk."

11

Olympia stepped back and stood in the doorway while Andrea spoke with the police. She did this as much to give the woman some privacy as to head off the girls if they decided they'd had enough of coloring and computer games. Careful to remain within hearing distance, she went into the kitchen to check out the food containers. They were still pretty hot. She found an assortment of chicken fingers and some brown rice, which were undoubtedly intended for the children. But further exploration revealed a container of vegetable pad Thai, a chicken curry, and a double order of spring rolls. Crises never affected Olympia's appetite, and she was getting hungrier by the minute. Still, out of deference to the situation, she would wait.

"Olympia?"

Andrea stood in the doorway holding the phone.

"The police want to come out here and talk to me tonight. Is that okay? I mean, I could go up there and meet them but…"

Olympia held up her hand. "Don't even think of it. You are not driving anywhere tonight. You are in shock, and it's snowing. If they want to talk to you that badly, they can damn well come here."

"But what about the girls? I don't want them to know yet. I don't want them to see their mother talking to the police."

Olympia stood and held out her hand for the phone. "May I speak to them?"

Andrea nodded and handed it over.

"Hello, Officer, this is Reverend Olympia Brown. I am the minister of the First Parish Church in Loring. Andrea Riggs and her two daughters are here with me in my home in Brookfields. It's just north of Plymouth."

"Thank you, ma'am. How did you know we were looking for her?"

. "We learned what happened on the evening news."

"How's she taking it?"

"She's just learned that her husband's been murdered. How do you think she'd take it?"

"Did she arrive today?"

"They're staying here with us. They got here yesterday. We…I heard it on the news. Andrea hadn't gotten back yet."

"That's a convenient coincidence."

Olympia was losing patience. "I don't think it is a convenient coincidence at all. How could she know what would happen? The important thing right now is that she and the children are safe and cared for here with us. She has twin six-year-old daughters, but they haven't been told yet. Can you hold off coming here until we get them into bed? I have a private office. You can meet in there if you'd like. No, they are not going anywhere. Hold on, please."

Olympia turned to Andrea. "What time do you think?"

"How about nine? They'll be well out by then."

"Dr. Riggs would like you to come at or a little after nine."

Olympia gave the woman on the other end of the line the street address then rang off. "We've got at least three hours before they get here. Do you need some time alone? I can feed the kids. I found the chicken things and the rice. I'm assuming those are for them."

Andrea's eyes spoke her gratitude. "That would be wonderful. Let's have them show me their tent and tell me about their day. Then if you could feed them, I'll go off and have myself a long hot shower." She paused and rubbed her chin. "I suppose I should be feeling sad or something, but I don't. I just feel kind of numb."

"Go have your shower." Olympia waved her off. Andrea stood and smiled in silent gratitude as the girls exploded into the sitting room. They pictures they'd made of the kitchen-table tent, upon which sat the bags and boxes containing their supper.

"Exit, stage left." Olympia put an arm around each girl. "Let's get these up on the refrigerator, and you can help me set out the things for supper."

IN THE CHURCH BASEMENT, Emilio was rapidly getting worse. After a few hours of fitful half-sleep, he was awakened with bouts of convulsive coughing and the pain of aching joints. When he did manage to drift off, even for a few minutes, the dreams were more troubling than his physical distress: long-forgotten memories of playing in the streets outside his home and high school soccer matches with his schoolmates then an abrupt dream pivot to the feeling of choking and drowning. He saw the face of his young wife when she died giving birth to the daughter his mother and sisters were now raising. Then something with claws was chasing him. He wrenched himself into full waking, pulled himself into a semi-upright position, and dragged the jumble of blankets around his shoulders. Sleep might be impossible, but at least sitting up made breathing a little easier.

12

The two police detectives, a man and a woman, arrived at Olympia's home shortly after nine. Upon entering the big, old-fashioned kitchen, they introduced themselves as Wanda Licowski and Gabriel English. Olympia shook each of their hands, gave them her own name, and took them directly into her office.

"You'll have total privacy here, and I'll even turn off the phone so you won't be disturbed. It's not fancy, but it does the trick."

As the detectives settled themselves into the two small armchairs that flanked the sofa she kept as a spare bed for unexpected guests, Olympia offered them coffee. They declined.

"In that case, I'll go and get Andrea."

"Thank you, Reverend." Detective Licowski had a warm and pleasant voice, and for some inexplicable reason, this surprised and comforted Olympia. Maybe this wouldn't be so awful after all.

She returned in minutes with Andrea, solemn faced, red eyed and still wearing a headscarf to cover her hair loss. The two officers rose instantly to their feet.

"Detectives Licowski and English, this is Dr. Andrea Riggs. Like her late husband, she is a medical doctor. She was here with me when she got the news, and at her request and as her minister, I will be staying here with her for the interview." Without waiting for a response, Olympia directed Andrea to an upholstered armchair and settled herself emphatically on an antique rocker that came with the house.

LATER, after the detectives left and Frederick was long abed, all that remained for the moment, at least, was to make some decisions about how and what to tell the children.

"How about a small brandy to help us think? Medicinal purposes, of course."

A weary and teary Andrea nodded yes and blew her nose.

Olympia returned with two crystal balloon snifters, each containing a small amber pool of French brandy, the last drops of a souvenir bottle from a trip to France. Andrea took a sniff and then a small sip.

"I just can't sit them down and tell them their father was murdered, Olympia. What do I say? I mean, truthfully, I'm glad to be rid of him, but I'd never wish this on him either. I'm a mess."

Olympia swirled and stared into her own brandy. "Were the children close to him?"

"Nobody was close to him. To be honest, they barely knew him."

"That could be said of a lot of professional men: always working long hours. Too busy for the family."

Andrea shook her head and stared at the floor.

"No, Olympia, I got the feeling that he just didn't like being around us. We made too much noise. We made messes. He was home less and less, and when he was, it was like walking on eggs. Anything would set him off."

"Is there a reason why you didn't say anything about this to the detectives?"

Andrea stared at the floor and lifted her hand to her head. "I guess the real answer is because I'm so totally ashamed of myself for getting myself into a situation like this... that, and I thought I was protecting the girls."

"Andrea. If what you say is true, and I have no reason to believe it isn't, you didn't cause this. You are a victim, and he is—was—a sadistic predator." She paused and took a different tack. "I'd be interested in what his colleagues in Boston thought of him. I don't suppose I'll ever know."

Andrea grimaced. "I just thought of something else. I suppose there'll have to be a funeral or something. That'll be a five-star farce if there ever was one. This just keeps getting worse."

"I can help you. I've done more than one awkward funeral in my life. There'll be time enough to decide what you want to do about that. It's telling the kids I'm concerned about. That's going to be the next hurdle."

"Oh, God, I just had another awful thought."

"What's that?"

"Those two detectives... the questions they were asking. You don't think they think I had anything to do with it, do you?"

Olympia waved away the thought. "They have to question everybody connected to the man. It's routine. The first person they question is the next of kin. It's about finding out information, looking for leads, and trying to get a more complete picture of the man. Dear God, woman. You were out buying clothes for your kids. If they really push you, you can show them sales slips with times and dates. You did keep them, didn't you?"

Andrea nodded. "But there's something I didn't tell them."

"And what's that?"

Andrea bit her lip and said in a low voice, "I didn't tell you either. The first thing I did, right after I got the car, I went back to the house. Oh, I called into the hospital to make sure he was still in Boston. He was. There were some things I needed, papers, documents, medications, personal stuff. It was late morning, and I was in and out of there in less than ten minutes, but my fingerprints are going to be all over everything."

"Andrea, it's your house. Your fingerprints are already all over everything. It would raise suspicion if they weren't. Nobody thinks you killed the man."

"But somebody killed him, Olympia. That's what I'm afraid of. Somebody did, and my question is, is that somebody going to come after me and the girls? The man was a monster, but there's somebody out there who hated him even more than I did."

Olympia didn't have an answer for that, so she did her best to calm the distraught woman. "Try and look at it this way. Other than those two police detectives, no one knows you're here, and no one can trace you. You are safe. Leave the detective work to the professionals, and let's concentrate on the here and now… and how and when you are going to tell the girls."

In the end, the two women decided that they would tell the children first thing in the morning and depending on how they reacted, take it from there.

2 December 1865

Much to the children's delight, it started to snow this afternoon while Susan and I were speaking at an abolitionist meeting. Needless to say, the children were beside themselves with excitement and most anxious to go home and play in it. We were delayed, however, when Reverend Richard Fewkes, our minister, took me aside with what he described as a most-

pressing request. After some social pleasantries, which included asking me where I would be spending the Christmas season, he told me of a runaway slave, a woman named Lottie, who was in need of a place to live. He explained it would be for some weeks or until such time as she found work. I asked him where she was living at present. He replied with a smile that she was at home with him and his wife, but the house was far too small to accommodate her for an extended stay. He respectfully waited for me to respond. I already knew I would say yes but felt it only fitting that I should speak with Susan and the children before taking in another lodger.

…More anon, LFW.

13

Andrea was up before daybreak and quietly padding around the kitchen in search of the coffee. Olympia and Frederick heard her but decided the woman probably needed some time alone. The two were immediately of one mind, and given the unexpected window of opportunity, they seized it. Earlier in their relationship, Olympia had resisted Frederick's multiple proposals of marriage right up to the last one.

Now, several contented years later, she was solidly in favor of the many and varied benefits of married life: shared meals and connubial bliss at regular intervals. Marriage was like travel, she told herself with a satisfied smirk. It broadened a person.

After breakfast, an exceptionally cheerful Frederick excused himself to get ready for work, and Andrea suggested to Olympia that they might as well call in the children and get it over with.

Olympia topped up both their coffees. "Let's all go into the sitting room."

The two women were still wearing their bathrobes. Olympia's old standby, her much-loved pink terrycloth robe, had seen better days. It was not a thing of beauty, but it was part of her personal history, and she planned to wear it until it completely disintegrated. And by the looks of it, the day was not far off. Andrea had a nightgown of Olympia's and a spare bathrobe belonging to Frederick, double belted to keep it from tripping her.

The girls were still in their oversized, make-do nighties. Two of Olympia's old tie-dyed T-shirts had been pressed into service, and the girls were thrilled with them. "Shades of my colorful past," she'd told them. The two children sat side by side on the sofa and pulled the already stretched-out garments down over their knees all the way to their toes, watching their mother. Like cats, they knew when something was amiss. Andrea pulled a chair up to the sofa and sat directly across from them with her hands folded and resting on her knees. Olympia was in her chair.

"Julianne, Marybeth, I have something very sad to tell you. A very bad thing happened to your father yesterday. He got hurt, and the doctors couldn't fix him, and…. and then he died."

The girls looked first at each other and then at their mother. Julianne was the first to speak. "Daddy? Died? Like when our old dog Sammy died, and we had to bury him in the backyard?"

Andrea nodded. "Sort of. Sammy was old. It was his time to die. This is different. Daddy had an accident, and it was so bad that the doctors couldn't fix him, and he died. But just like old Sammy, once you die, you don't come back."

"Can we go see him?"

Andrea shot a desperate look toward Olympia. Without missing a beat, Olympia picked up the thread.

"When a person dies, sometimes you can go see them, and sometimes you can't. There's a lot we don't know yet, honey. But when we find out, we'll tell you. Promise."

Marybeth nodded but looked doubtful. Neither of them

openly cried. They just sat, wide-eyed and uncharacteristically quiet, unsure of what to do next.

Olympia watched the two children and wondered why they were so calm. What were they thinking? On the other hand, what did she expect? Even for a minister, she was in unchartered territory.

"Would you like to tell me about your daddy?" asked Olympia.

"He worked a lot." Julianne poked her toes in and out from under the stretched-out shirt.

"He was a doctor," said Marybeth.

"Did you like to do things with him?"

"He was always working. He didn't do things with us."

"Would you like to draw a picture of him for me sometime? I never met your father, so I don't know what he looked like," said Olympia.

Silence.

"Maybe later," said Julianne.

"What kind of accident?"

Andrea shot a desperate look at Olympia.

"We're not exactly sure yet, honey. People are trying to find that out right now, and I promise the minute we know for sure, we'll talk to you. Can that be okay for now?"

Julianne nodded and twirled a strand of hair.

"I have to go to the bathroom," said Marybeth.

"Me too."

Andrea rubbed her forehead. "Tell you what. Why don't you two take yourselves upstairs and get dressed? There's still some clean clothes in your backpacks, and I put the things I bought yesterday on top of the chest at the end of the bed."

"Can't we just go home?" Julianne was beginning to whine.

Andrea shook her head and looked into their two questioning faces. "Not today," she whispered.

When the children left the room, Andrea turned to

Olympia. "If there's any way I can manage it, I'm never setting foot in that place again. I hated it when he bought it, and the way I feel right now, I don't think I could even stand to look at a picture of it. I came close to throwing up just walking into it to get my stuff." She stopped and stood. "Enough! I need to get dressed myself. It's going to be a long day."

Olympia waited until Andrea came back downstairs before going off to work. She kept finding piddly little things to do around the kitchen. Stalling really. In truth, she was worried and not terribly happy about leaving Andrea and the girls alone, despite the fact that Andrea seemed more focused and in control of herself after talking with the girls.

Olympia knew there was more to the story, much more, but it was not her place to ask. At least, not yet. She folded and put away a dish towel and hit the Start button on the dishwasher. There was nothing left to do but give Andrea what she hoped was a comforting hug and leave.

"Don't push yourself, Andrea. I'll be back as soon as I can, and we can take it from there."

"Take what from where?"

"Oh, hell, I don't know any more than you do. I'm just trying to say the right thing."

Andrea smiled. "Go to work, Olympia. I'll be all right. And if I'm not, I know exactly where to find you. Remember?"

Olympia gave her a thumbs-up. "Point made. See you by mid-afternoon at the latest."

Inside her van, Olympia turned the key and shivered. Old VWs, while quirky and cranky and much beloved by their similarly attributed and devoted owners, were absolute stinkers to heat. Anything that even remotely passed for heat would not kick in for at least twenty minutes. And that would only be enough to keep your blood from freezing. They were, however, absolutely dependable. The grand old lady coughed gently, sputtered, and then lumbered down the driveway. The snowfall of the night before had not been a major event. A few inches lay on the level areas and outlined some of the trees, but the roads were clear, and driving would not be a problem.

Out on the main road, Olympia slipped her brain into autopilot mode and reached for her travel mug. The warmth in her free hand was comforting. She took an appreciative sip and continued to drive with the cold hand on the steering wheel. The trick was to finish the coffee before it froze. Now, in this beautiful clear morning after the first snow of the winter, she let her thoughts drift back to the police interview of the night before.

The two detectives had asked Andrea all the predicable questions: did Dr. Cabot have any enemies? None that she knew of. Did the man drink to excess? Not really. Were there financial problems? He kept the books. If there were financial issues, she would never know. Were they having domestic problems? Olympia remembered that Andrea hesitated before responding to that one. Finally, she'd said that every couple has differences, and they weren't any different. Then she added that James found it hard to find a balance between work and family and that it seemed to get worse after the girls came along.

Wanda Licowski had picked up on that and pressed her about "having problems." Andrea nodded in response but offered nothing more.

The two took turns asking questions about her husband, his work, and his habits, many of which she couldn't answer. If they found that to be curious, they didn't say, but they did write everything down. All in all, the whole thing seemed very civilized to Olympia, the observer. On the other hand, what did she know? This was not the first murder investigation she'd been involved in, and given her nose for finding troubled souls, it would not likely be her last.

A flashing yellow light ahead of her pulled her back into the moment. Daydreaming and internal monologues were often part of her day, but left unattended, they could be dangerous to her health, especially when she was driving. She signaled and pulled out onto the highway heading north, finished the coffee without spilling any of it, and drifted back to thoughts about the previous evening and her growing admiration for Andrea.

She's doing remarkably well, considering. But considering what? There were several pieces to this unfolding puzzle that either didn't fit or were entirely missing.

Forty-eight hours ago, a woman she'd never seen before came into the church seeking help. Was she seeking sanctuary from the abuse or… Olympia grimaced and tried to push away the dreadful thought. Was the woman, in fact, creating an alibi? She shook her head. Andrea was fearful and desperate, but certainly not, in Olympia's years of experience with unhappy people, a killer. There was no doubt going to be more to this unfortunate business. But what was it going to be, and was it really her job to find out?

She was well aware that she had a bit of a knack for this sort of thing, for sorting through difficult and even unlawful situations. Some would call it snooping or sticking her nose in where it didn't belong. The question was, and continued to be over the years, did she—should she—get personally involved? Too late. *So stop dithering and admit it, Olympia. You're in for the long haul.*

14

Olympia signaled and turned left into the church parking lot. Franklin Bowen was outside stringing Christmas lights along the bushes that framed the building. She waved. He nodded. Franklin was a man of few words, who she was still trying to figure out. Would he by an ally or a stone wall or a little of each? She wasn't sure.

The snow on the church roof and on the trees looked so beautiful. She wondered when or if the plow would come. Was there even enough to plow? Maybe the church fathers and mothers should try and save a few dollars by simply waiting and letting nature take its course. She shrugged. Not her problem—at least not today.

Olympia crunched her way to the door, grateful it wasn't slippery, and looked again. She saw what looked like bicycle tracks, almost erased by the wind. Who the hell would be riding a bike in the snow? She pushed open the door, made straight for her office, and pushed up the thermostat.

The building's interior was warmer than the outside, but not by much. Still wearing her coat and hat, she went into the sanctuary and up the center aisle to the pulpit to retrieve her personal hymnbook. As well as the regular Sunday service, she also needed to get a start on the Christmas Eve service.

She was rummaging around the lectern when she heard an odd scraping sound. Must be a creaky board, she told herself, but not one I'm familiar with. She listened for a repeat but heard nothing. By now, she was on a first-name basis with the grunts, groans, squeaks, and squawks of the old church, and this was not one of them.

"Never mind." She closed the door behind her and headed back into the comforting warmth of her office. "It's probably just the wind coming from a different direction. There's no one here but me."

GORDON BENNETT, the church administrator, wasn't due in until ten that morning, which meant Olympia had a few minutes to herself to get the nuts and bolts of the paperwork out of the way. The first step in the process was to nail down the sermon title. Everything else in the service needed to relate to the topic, and at the moment, while her mind spun with what was happening at home, the sermon-title section of her brain was totally blank.

Coffee! It was the universal cure-all and personal theological stimulant. She headed out to the kitchen to make some and was surprised to find a couple of the cabinet doors standing open. One of the unbreakable rules of church life is that if you use the kitchen, you clean the kitchen. She pushed them shut and once again thanked the inventor of the one-cup-at-a-time coffee maker. Yes, the magical device was environmentally wasteful, but there were times, and this was one of them, when she set her principles aside and went straight for the caffeine.

Back in her office with the steaming, fragrant coffee in front of her, she was mentally sifting through possible sermon topics when she heard the outside door open followed by the sound of footsteps coming down the hall. She knew it wasn't Gordy. By now, Olympia knew the sound pattern of his footsteps. Well then, who was it? Another pastoral emergency? Please, no. She looked up and saw one of the church matriarchs, Patricia Besom, Mrs. B., as she was affectionately called by everyone who came through the door. By the look of her, she was a woman on a mission.

Olympia did her best to look pleased. She liked Mrs. Besom. True, the woman could be overly direct. She was also sometimes surreptitiously called Madame DeFarge because of her constant and ever-present knitting. Reputation notwithstanding, Olympia had a genuine fondness for the woman. She'd figured out early on that, for all her sharp-tongued bluster, Mrs. Besom was a highly intelligent force to be reckoned with…and a heart as big as her knitting bag.

A welcoming smile spread across Olympia's face as she stood to welcome the woman. Even more than the church administrator, Mrs. Besom knew where the bodies were buried. She also knew how they'd gotten there and who'd buried them.

"Hey, look what the snow blew in. What brings you to church on a cold and frosty morning?" Olympia liked sprinkling lines of familiar poetry, folksongs, and Shakespeare into her speech and sermons—the Bible, not so much. "You're looking good today. I've just made some coffee. Can I make you a cup?"

Mrs. Besom was catching her breath from walking in the cold and unwinding several layers of one of her hand-knitted scarves when the two women heard something outside in the hallway: a scraping, foot- dragging sound followed by a strangled cough.

Without thinking, Olympia ran past Mrs. Besom into the hallway to find a man staggering toward her. She instantly recognized the young Brazilian man who sometimes slipped into the back of the church on a Sunday morning. *His name, what's his name?* He sometimes stayed for coffee. *Emilio, that's it!* She realized she didn't know his last name. He was gray-faced and gasping for breath as he croaked out the words, "*Por favor, Senhora, me ajude…* uh please help me… I…." He stumbled then crumpled onto the floor.

Olympia gasped and started to run forward, but Mrs. B. caught her by the arm.

"You call 911. I'll stay with him. I used to be an EMT before I started knitting."

Olympia raced past Mrs. B., never so grateful in her life to have this enigmatic wisewoman by her side and on her side. After making the call, Olympia ran back out into the hallway. Mrs. Besom had already thrown her own sweater under the young man and rolled him onto his side to ease his breathing and keep him from choking.

"Get me some water, a spoon, and a wet cloth and some ice." Mrs. Besom stroked the young man's forehead. "He's burning up, and he's dehydrated."

By the time Olympia returned with the water, they could already hear the wailing howl of the approaching ambulance. Mrs. B. looked at her watch. "Under five minutes. Not bad. Do you want to go with him? I think somebody should. You can leave your car here, and I'll lock up the church. Once he's settled and stabilized, you can call me, and I'll come and get you. South Coast General is less than twenty minutes from here. It won't be a problem."

"God love you," said Olympia as the EMTs ran through the door.

"Somebody's got to," quipped Mrs. B., hauling herself to her feet and moving out of the way.

The next few minutes were a well-orchestrated fast-action scene that would have done justice to any TV hospital reality show. The medics arrived and went into action. In less than two minutes, the young man, Emilio, was strapped onto a gurney and being rolled out the door toward the waiting ambulance.

"Mrs. B., do you think you could stay here and wait for Gordy and tell him what happened? He should be here any minute."

"No problem. I've got my knitting, and I know where to find the teapot. I'll be fine. You go do what needs to be done, Reverend. I've got this."

Olympia blew the woman a grateful kiss, ran out the door, and climbed into the ambulance. Once inside, she twisted around so she could see. He was wound into a tangle of tubes and wires, and he looked awful, helpless, frightened, and in pain.

"He's in your hands, God. Do your best, will you?" she whispered.

"You say something to me?" asked the driver.

"I was saying a prayer for the man back there."

He nodded and stepped on the gas. "Can't hurt."

15

When they arrived, the hospital staff wasted no time getting Emilio out of the ambulance and into a cubicle. After pulling the curtains around him, they directed Olympia back to the waiting room. She wasn't family, they said, so she couldn't stay. Even claiming to be his minister didn't work. It usually did. Grumbling to herself, Olympia went out into a brightly decorated, cheerless room, picked up a limp copy of *Time Magazine*, and looked at her watch.

While waiting, she telephoned into the church office and updated Gordy on where she was and what she was doing there. But when he asked how he had come to be in the church in the first place, Olympia realized she hadn't a clue. She was so busy tending to the man that she'd not given that aspect of the situation a single thought.

"He must have come in after I got there," she said, remembering the windswept, almost pristine snow in the parking lot. "Otherwise, he couldn't have gotten in, could he? The door was locked, remember. It's a good thing he did, though, and he's lucky we were there."

"Mrs. B. was here when I came in to work. She told me what happened. She's a mystery, that one. Tough as nails on the outside, and yet there's a real soft side to her that most people don't know about."

Not that much of a mystery, thought Olympia. Mrs. B. wasn't the first, nor would she be the last gentle person to protect herself from the slings and arrows of the less kind.

"Ma'am? Are you the person who came in with Emilio Vieira?" Olympia looked up to see a young man in blue hospital scrubs coming toward her.

"I have to go, Gordy. I think they are going to let me go see him."

When she entered the room, Emilio opened his eyes and looked at her. She saw neither welcome nor relief in his eyes. She saw fear. He looked like a cornered animal. Trapped. He was wound into almost as many electronic monitors and devices as he had been in the ambulance. She was relieved to see that his color was distinctly better, and with the constant flow of oxygen, he was no longer fighting to breathe.

Olympia approached but stopped a short distance away and looked kindly at the man in the bed. She spoke softly. "I don't know what made you think to come to us, Emilio, but I can only say, thank God you did. We will help you however we can."

"You call police?" he croaked.

Olympia shook her head and waved away the question. "Oh, God, no. Why would I do that? You didn't do anything wrong. You came to a church in need of help. I'm glad you did. I never knew that Mrs. B. used to be an EMT. She knew exactly what to do."

"You not call police?"

"Emilio, I did not call the police. You are very sick. That is not against the law."

He was clearly agitated, twisting his fingers and picking at the wires that connected him to the machines. "My papers— visa not good. They come, they send me back. My baby…"

The fearsome light bulb flashed inside Olympia's head,

and the picture cleared. Of course. He's undocumented. Now what? Think fast.

She walked up to the side of the bed and held out her hand. Slowly, he reached up and took it. "Emilio, I did not, and I will not tell the police anything. There isn't any need to. If anyone does ask, I will say that you go to my church. This morning, you were very sick, and you came into the church looking for help, and we called an ambulance. I am the minister. I've seen you in church. You always sit in the back. I'll tell the doctors I know you. I'll even tell them you do some work at the church. I've seen you carry chairs and move tables. That's work, isn't it?"

Never in her life had Olympia seen such a welling up of gratitude and relief suffuse a human face. She gave his hand a little squeeze. Now, they were both weepy-eyed.

When he found his voice, he whispered, "Pneumonia. I have no money for hospital... I can't stay."

She shook her head.

"You can stay. They have to treat you. It's the law. They can't say no. Anyway, we'll talk about that later. First things first. You need to get better, and then we can take you out of here. Where do you live?"

Emilio looked away and muttered, "With friends."

"Can you tell me where?"

He was starting drift off. "I think they move. Not tell me."

"You sleep," she whispered. "I'll come back later." Outside the door, she marched down the wide and white corridor and headed straight for the nurses' station. There, she identified herself as Emilio's minister and part-time employer and gave them her contact information.

The next step was lunch and a call to Father Jim—in that order. She was starving. After she put something into her grumbling stomach, she would call her priest friend and see what he could tell her about immigration law. Not that he was an immigration specialist, far from it. But he had contacts, useful, powerful contacts that went back to his childhood playmates in the West End of Boston and then expanded and solidified when he worked as a parish priest in solidly Irish-Catholic Dorchester. A priest who worked hand in glove with the local police and knew how to keep his mouth shut was a valuable asset. For years, Jim had been her go-to person when she had legal or procedural questions. He was her personal sounding board and reflecting mirror. If Jim didn't have the answers, he usually knew where to find them.

LATER, sitting at an orange Formica table at a McDonald's directly across the street from the hospital, Olympia felt better. She had just finished off a modest salad and washed it down with a monstrous strawberry shake, whipped cream and all. Now, she could take on the world. She pulled out her cell phone and hit speed dial.

"Jim?"

"Uh-oh. I know that tone of voice. What—or more likely who—is it this time?"

"No surprises for you anymore, eh? We've known each other for too long, and actually, it's a two-fer. But I'll start with the most pressing issue. What do you know about immigration law? There's an undocumented man, a Brazilian, in South Coast General Hospital suffering from pneumonia. He collapsed in my church this morning. I went with him in the ambulance. He's in the ICU right now, but I think he'll be all right. As far as I know, he has no one here to help him, and he's terrified of being deported. He mentioned a baby. I'm going back after I talk to you and see what more I can learn. He trusted me enough to come into the church for help. That, at least, is a starting point."

Jim groaned audibly on the other side of the line. "Okay,

that's one. Might as well get it all out, Olympia. Who's the other one?"

"It's a long story."

"What's the short version?"

"On Tuesday, I took a woman and her twin daughters home to stay with us until she got herself sorted out. The day after she moved in—that would be yesterday—I learned on the evening news that her husband was found shot to death outside his home in Loring by the Sea…not three streets away from the church."

A pause. "Jesus, Olympia. You don't fool around, do you? How well do you know these two people?"

"The Brazilian man has come to the church a few times. Before today, I didn't really know him other than to say hello. He was always very polite. The woman literally walked in off the street and into the church with her two little girls. She was a mess, battered and terrified. Her husband had actually pulled out some of her hair. She told me she lived there in town, and she looked like she was running for her life." A pause. "I guess she was."

"Where are you now?"

"In a McDonald's across from the hospital."

"How much time do you have? Can you give me all the details about the Brazilian man? I might as well start there."

"His name is Emilio. Like I said, he's Brazilian. He has a baby back in Brazil. He's overstayed his visa, and he's terrified of being deported. That's about it. He was pretty groggy. I'm going to try and find out more when I go back."

"Okay, that is something at least. I'll go see my old buddy, Jerry O'Brien, at the Dorchester Police Station and ask if he might have names, or know where to find names of an immigration lawyer and/or some immigrant advocate groups. Until we know the status of his papers and the type of visa he let lapse, there's not much we can do. As long as you're in contact with him, we at least have a starting point. What about the woman and the kids?"

"They're with me, and they're out of harm's way. The police are handling the legalities and the investigation of the death. They came to my house and talked to her last night. The man was shot, point-blank, several times and pronounced dead when the ambulance arrived. The police didn't tell us anything we hadn't already learned on the news report. The widow and the children are staying with Frederick and me."

"You said twins, right? You've got yourself a houseful, haven't you?"

"They're no trouble. The kids are adorable, and their mother is amazing. I have no idea how she's managing to hold it all together. We're just glad we were at the right place at the right time and that she said yes to the offer of coming home with me. God knows, we've got the room."

"You are the one who's amazing, Olympia. Minister and earth-mother-hen all rolled up into one."

"That's me, all right, and I've got the scars to prove it." She laughed, feeling less alone and more confident now that she'd enlisted Jim. "Thank you, my friend. I'm going back to the hospital. I'll call you when I know more."

16

When she returned, the medical staff told her Emilio was responding well but would be in the hospital for at least two or three more days and asked if she knew where he lived. Olympia said she did not but would try and find out.

Olympia entered the room and asked Emilio's permission to sit beside the bed and if he was feeling better. He nodded. Then, bit by bit, as they talked, she slowly learned more about his personal history. She asked gentle questions and eventually learned that his wife had died in childbirth, and his baby daughter was being cared for by his mother back in Brazil. He told her that before he left home, he'd been a teacher at a small college, but the pay was terrible. Shortly after his wife died, he came to the States on a travel visa. Once here, he began working all the hours he could get and sending every cent back to his mother, his baby, and his two sisters.

He asked Olympia to get his wallet out of the bedside table drawer and showed Olympia a picture of a dimpled, dark-haired, giggling baby girl.

"This is my Gisela." His voice broke. He coughed, swallowed, and closed his eyes for a few seconds while Olympia sat in pastoral silence beside him. "She walk soon. She grow so fast."

"She's very beautiful, Emilio, and I think she looks a lot like her daddy."

"No, like her mother."

As they talked, a slow trust began to grow. Emilio finally told her the name of the restaurant where he worked, The Windjammer, and asked if she would call the manager and tell him he was sick and to please let him keep his job. He would come back to work as soon as he could.

"You need to get well first, Emilio. You do that for yourself and for Gisela. I will call your manager."

"He's a good man."

At the end of the visit, after promising to return tomorrow, she left the room and called Mrs. B. for the promised ride.

"I'll be standing inside the entrance to the visitor's parking lot. It's out of the wind, and it will be easier for you to pull over and pick me up."

Then what? Olympia asked herself. Of course, the woman would be curious to know how the young man was doing. But how much should she say? The trick would be to tell Mrs. B. enough to satisfy her curiosity but not enough to betray anything of the confidence she'd just managed to earn. Mrs. B. had a good-heart. Olympia knew that, but where did she stand on the immigration issue? On illegals? On undocumented foreigners? On strangers with brown skin? She knew well that people in the "land of opportunity" were often sharply divided on the subject. Her mother often said, "The less said, the less mended," and sometimes, Olympia heard the message. She would speak only of his improving health.

A quick bright *toot* from an approaching car startled Olympia and yanked her hard back into the here and now of a freezing cold parking garage on a windy December day.

Mrs. B. waved, pulled over, and Olympia slid in, glad to be in a warm car with a kindly lady.

"How's the patient?"

"He'll be there for a couple of days, but he's going to be okay."

"Did you find out any more about him?"

"Yes and no. I'm going to have to claim pastoral privilege here. Let's just say, it's complicated."

"Not surprising. These people come here looking for the American Dream, and just as often, it turns into a nightmare."

Olympia said nothing.

"And talk about complicated… How about the murder of that Dr. James Cabot? I suppose you've heard of it by now? Loring by the Sea is supposed to be a sleepy little town where nothing bad ever happens."

"I heard it on the news last night," said Olympia. "It's horrible. I didn't know the man, but it makes me think twice about being alone in the church."

"I don't think anybody knew him. He didn't practice here in town, and when he was here, he kept to himself. So did the wife. He was part of a big group of specialists in Boston. Very prestigious, I hear." She shrugged. "Lot of good it did him."

"Mmmmm."

Mrs. B. stopped in the church parking lot and said her goodbyes. Olympia again expressed her gratitude for everything and waved her off.

She was relieved to see Gordy's car was still there. She had more questions to ask, and she knew from past experience that the most reliable source of local history, news, information, and sometimes, juicy gossip was invariably the church administrator. These people, mostly women and usually town residents, knew everyone in the church and in the surrounding town. You could learn a lot in a church—sometimes more than you wanted to know. Too much information.

Most people didn't know that. Olympia knew it all too well and used it to her advantage as needed.

The parking lot had been plowed, but there were still icy patches underfoot. Olympia walked carefully to the side door of the church and tried to push it open. When it didn't budge, she dug her key out of her pocket and using it to gain entrance, she called out a cheery but weary "Hello" as she entered the building.

Bennett called back from the office and asked Olympia to please lock the door behind her. Olympia did so and wondered about the change. The church doors were usually left open during the day as long as there was someone in the building. It was not as though they worried about theft or vandalism or anything. Then she remembered. Yesterday, not three streets away from where she was standing, a man, a prestigious doctor, had been shot to death in his own back-yard. And the victim's wife, who might or might not be a suspect in the murder, was living in sanctuary in Olympia's own home. Was this a blessed coincidence, or was the universe playing a really dirty cosmic trick on her—and would she ever find out?

She rounded the corner and stepped into the outer office to find Gordy staring at his computer.

"Don't mind me. I was just checking to see if there's any more on the murder." He made a face. "I don't mind telling you this thing has shut down the whole town. Everyone's on guard, looking over their shoulder, locking their cars and their doors and their windows. It's giving me the creeps just thinking about it."

Olympia pulled off her coat and scarf, tossed the tangle over a nearby chair, and sat down in another one.

"Did you know either of them, the doctor or his wife?"

Gordy shook his head. "Wouldn't know them if I fell over them. They kept to themselves. Everybody I know thought they were a little strange. They never joined in with anything in town. Heck, I'm not sure they even voted. We used to see her with the kids once in a while. Twins, you know. Two little girls. We'd see her pushing them in one of those double stroller things. That must have been some hard work going up hills and such. Anyway, they never socialized in town, never joined a church—not that I know of anyway—and now this. They say she was a doctor too, but she never practiced. Maybe it was because of the kids. Twins will keep you real busy." Gordy rolled his eyes and chuckled. "One of my sisters had twins. Almost did her in. We all helped out when they were little. Uh….sorry. What were you asking?"

Olympia smiled. "I was asking if you knew the family."

"Guess I gave you the long answer. The short answer is no. Why?"

"Just curious. You were checking the news. Do they have any idea who might have done it?"

"Nothing yet, but people in town are talking about seeing a stranger riding a bicycle around here sometimes. They've seen him near the library too, and somebody said she thought she'd seen him at night right here near the church. We're only three streets away from where it happened. I'll tell you, I'm locking all doors until they find him. My house, my car, and this place too. You can't be too careful. Good heavens, I never thought I'd hear myself say something like that in a place like this. Makes you wonder, doesn't it?"

"It certainly does," said Olympia, careful not to give any indication of exactly what it made her wonder. "It's been quite a day, and I still need to make some phone calls. Say, you don't know anyone local with a room to rent, do you?"

"Who's looking?"

"The man who took sick today. He may have lost his housing. I'm not sure. His name is Emilio Vieira. He's from Brazil. He's come to church a couple of times on Sundays. Good thing he thought to come here. He was in bad shape. I got to know a little bit about him in the hospital. He said he had a job and was living with friends, but that kind of situation can be chancy."

"What do you mean?"

"Well, from what I've heard, a lot of them end up with unscrupulous landlords putting too many people in a room, rent gouging, unhealthy living conditions…."

Gordon rolled his eyes. "They bring it on themselves, you know."

Olympia let her questioning look speak for her.

"You're not going to like hearing me say this, being a minister and all, but these people sneak in here, live under the radar, sponge off the system, don't pay taxes, get into trouble, and they expect us to foot the bill and bail them out. I mean, there's helping people who deserve it, and there's helping people who don't deserve it. You gotta make a choice. I don't believe in free rides, Reverend Olympia. You have to work for what you get. At least that's how I was brought up." He was getting red in the face, and his voice got louder.

"We all make choices." Olympia rose from the chair and gathered up her things. "As I said, I need to make some phone calls and then go make a home visit to the Wilsons."

Gordy was instantly concerned. "Something wrong? I sure hope not. They're such a wonderful family."

"Well it's no secret that they're moving to another state. I thought I'd drop in and check in with them, see how they're doing. Moving is so unsettling. Maybe go see if there was anything the church could do to help."

"Well make sure you tell them to lock their doors at night. They live one street away from where the murder happened. Probably a good thing they're moving."

"Absolutely," said the Reverend Doctor Olympia Brown. "You can't be too careful these days."

17

L oring PD Detectives, Gabe English and Wanda Licowski, approached the main desk at Mercy Hospital in Boston's Longwood medical district. Wanda made the introductions.

"Excuse me, ma'am. We're investigating the murder of Dr. James Cabot. I wonder if you could direct us to someone who might be willing to sit down for a few minutes and talk with us."

The pink-shirted, gray-haired woman behind the desk fidgeted with a paperclip and looked uncomfortable. "Um... we can't talk about patients or staff. There's a ..."

Licowski held up her hand. "We know about the HIPPA law and patient privacy, ma'am. Don't worry. This is police business. We're just trying to get a better picture of the man — you know, where he worked, who he worked with. Background information, nothing personal. We are trying to put together a picture of who he was so we can work on finding out who killed him."

More fidgeting. "I'm only a volunteer here, and this is the front desk. We don't know anything about.... He has....uh... he had an office up on the cardiology unit, seventh floor." Her voice sounded stronger now that she'd figured out a way to get them away from her desk. "Take the elevator and follow the signs. There's a department administrator on the desk there who can tell you way more than I can." She smiled uncertainly and pointed toward the elevator. "Remember, seventh floor, turn left when you get out, and follow the signs."

When the two detectives reached the Cardiology unit, the teary-eyed woman behind the desk held a crumpled Kleenex in one hand and poked at the papers on her desk with the other. Wanda repeated the question almost verbatim, that as part of their investigation into the man's murder, if there might be someone in the department who knew or worked with Dr. Cabot who might have time to speak with them, it would be much appreciated.

The red-faced woman asked them to please take a seat and explained that the department was in complete chaos, but she would see what she could do. She returned shortly and said if they didn't mind waiting for a few minutes, Dr. Patel, one of the other specialists in the unit, would see them in his office.

A few minutes later, a young man in blue scrubs escorted them through the door and into the clinical area. He led them past several examination rooms to a cluster of small offices at the end of the hall and opened one of the doors. "Sir, madam, this is Dr. Revi Patel, the acting chief cardiologist. He was a close associate of Dr. Cabot."

Dr. Patel looked up, adjusted his glasses, waved them in, but did not come out from behind his desk. "Come in please, and if you don't mind, close the door behind you. I don't mind saying this has devastated all of us. Jim Cabot was a brilliant man. I don't know what I can tell you, but I'll do my best to help." The man was sharp-eyed, brown-skinned, and appeared to be slight of stature. He spoke in the musical, singsong speech patterns of people from the South Asian

Continent when he welcomed them and directed them to their seats. There was nothing small or slight in his presence or demeanor, and Detectives Licowski and English did as they were told and learned absolutely nothing.

LATER, on the way back to Loring PD headquarters, the two detectives reviewed the lackluster and uninformative conversation with Dr. Patel. Gabe, who was not driving, took notes as they inched south out of Boston. Despite the expressway prime-time traffic channeling, and the use of an HOV lane, exiting the city at rush hour was a test of anyone's driving mettle.

"Well, that was a whole lot of big words that said zip on a shingle," said Gabe.

Wanda nodded, keeping her eyes on the road, watching for any movement or opening that might advance their journey through the tangled maze. "Yeah. Brilliant doctor, kept to himself, highly respected, didn't know him other than at work, in other words, 'We don't disrespect our colleagues, and you're not getting anything out of us.' The medical code of silence in full operation." She snorted in exasperation.

"To say anything less would make the hospital look bad. That's not gonna happen. People stick together. What did you expect? We're no better, you know."

She nodded. "I know, but there was a whole lot that wasn't being said in there. The pauses and hesitations, the sideways glances said it all. I can only hope that someone decides to break rank and come forward."

"Right, and pigs fly." Gabe pocketed the notepad and pencil.

"No so fast, there. We've done this before. Give 'em some time to think. Give us some time to dig up more evidence, and then we go back to the hospital and approach it from another angle. My gut is telling me something's going on there. Something's got our Dr. Patel and his friends very eager to be rid of us, something the man does not want to talk about that might be very, very messy."

"And we all know about your indisputable gut-radar." Gabe laughed and patted his stomach. "When I get signals like that, it's usually gas."

Wanda groaned and rolled her eyes. "And then there's the beautiful and not-so-very-tearful widow. She wasn't telling us everything either."

"They never do, at least not at the beginning. We'll get there. She'll come around."

"You think she did it."

"No, I don't. But that doesn't say she didn't have something to with it. She's not a happy lady, and I don't think her recent bereavement is what's causing it. Spouses have, in the past, arranged for the offing of a spouse they wanted to be rid of. I know misery and fear when I see it, and last night, we were looking at both of them right in the face. Her face."

Wanda nodded and swerved hard into an opening in the lane beside them.

"Nice move, woman! We'll get there eventually. It's just a question of when and what we're gonna find when we do. Right now, nothing is adding up. Big famous doctor is shot is his backyard for no apparent reason. But we know there's always a reason. Random shootings don't usually happen in pricey, suburban backyards. Whoever he was went to the house, went around to the back, and the victim opened the door. Remember, there was no sign of forced entry."

"So you think a man did the shooting."

Gabe nodded. "Oh, yeah. Women don't operate that way. This was well planned, vicious, and close range. Somebody knew where he lived and knew when he'd be there."

"Or followed him."

"Point."

"And right now, that's where the trail ends." She tapped the steering wheel in frustration.

"Meanwhile, we follow up on the tip about the dark-skinned stranger on the bicycle back in town."

"I thought about that. Strangers are always suspect."

Gabe nodded. "True…and it could also be a xenophobic BWB reaction."

"BWB?"

"Biking while black…or brown. Same as DWB, driving while black. Loring is super lily-white, and they are predictably suspicious of strangers. A dark-skinned stranger on a bike could be anyone. It could be nothing, a coincidence, or it could be somebody keeping track of the victim. Either way, we have to check it out."

Wanda held up a finger. "Wait a minute. Didn't a 911 call come in the other day for some guy who took sick at the local church?"

"You're right. They took him to the hospital. Never heard anything more, so I guess he didn't die. When we get back, I'll check the report for a description. If he's still there, we can go see for ourselves. That's a long shot. How many murderers go looking for help in a church?"

He nodded. "Meanwhile, Detective Licowski, I think it's time we go to that very church and see what we can learn from the kindly reverend, who I understand accompanied him to the ER."

"When did we go all formal? Something I said?"

He shook his head and laughed. "Nah, just checking to see if you were listening."

"Shithead!"

"You're welcome!"

18

The call Detective Gabe English was hoping would come, came on Saturday. The caller, who of course, would not give his name, said he was a colleague of Jim Cabot's, and he'd been at the hospital when the detectives had come in, but despite his offer and willingness to do so, he had not been allowed to meet with them.

"In fact," said the caller, "I was basically ordered to get the hell out of there. The morning after the murder, we were all called in for a meeting and told, as a group, we were to say absolutely nothing to the police or the press about Jim, about his practice, or anything remotely related to him. If anyone approached us, we were to refer them to Dr. Patel. That's when I knew I had to come forward. There's some bad stuff going on in here."

The detective scribbled notes as quickly as his fingers would move. In minutes, they agreed, under guarantee of anonymity, to meet later that day, well outside of Boston and nowhere near Loring by the Sea. They eventually decided on a café in Quincy Center, across from the historic President's Church and agreed not to wear their uniforms and to drive an unmarked car.

"Would you say this guy's a little paranoid?" asked Wanda.

"Overly cautious, perhaps. His reputation could be on the line if he's found out."

"Or his job."

"Or worse, if Dr. Cabot is an example."

She bit her lip and nodded.

"I gather he didn't say who he was. You gonna trace the call?"

Gabe answered this with a dark look over his glasses. "Of course, but I'll lay money he used a public phone. There are one or two of those left, you know."

"Makes you think, doesn't it?"

"In this business, my friend, everything makes you think."

THE COFFEE SHOP-CAFÉ was about as ordinary as white bread and butter. Housed in an old building, it had well-worn wood floors, exposed brick walls, long, tall windows on either side of the door, and an embossed tin ceiling. The place had been there for years. At two in the afternoon, there were very few people who would notice or remember the man and woman who entered and took a table near the back. Nor would they remember the tall, African American man who joined them minutes later. The three sat well away from the windows and ordered coffees all around.

Once they were seated and their orders taken, the informant opened the conversation. "Look, I'm putting my career and possibly even my life in your hands with what I'm going to tell you. But before I say one word, I need your word one more time that you will guarantee to keep my name out of it."

"We can do that. With two of us here, one will verify the other if it comes to that. A man's been murdered. We want to find out why, and we want to find the person who did it. You told me you had some information."

The man nodded and introduced himself. "I'm Darnel Lincoln. I worked with Jim, and...well, I might as well get straight to the point."

"Excuse me, Dr. Lincoln, but we'd like to record this conversation. Do we have your permission?"

Lincoln hesitated, clearly doubtful.

"We can always distort your voice if it comes to that."

H shook his head. "I'd rather you didn't, so...no."

"I will take notes then, and I'll show them to you before we leave. How's that?"

He nodded. "Jim was a brilliant cardiologist, one of the best in the world. That's documented. He's saved any number, maybe hundreds, of people's lives. The thing is, over the last couple of years, he started to change. Not his practice or his techniques, not at the beginning anyway, but we were all beginning to notice things."

"What kinds of things?"

"Well, he was never sociable. We chalked that up to his brilliance...you know, the odd-mannered-genius type? We just accepted it as who he was."

Wanda nodded, and Gabe scribbled notes.

"He was always kind of moody, but about a year and a half ago, it started getting worse, much worse. It's like he turned into two different people. He was losing weight too. Then he started making mistakes, first little ones, then big ones, but everybody covered for him. Nothing was ever said. It was just expected, and we fell into line. He was the hospital's shining star, and we needed to do our own work. We were still saving lives."

If any of this was shocking or disturbing to the two detectives, they did not let it show. They'd heard worse.

Lincoln continued. "Then someone in the department reported that drugs were going missing. At first, they tried to cover that up too, but it was getting worse. I started putting two and two together. Cabot had all the symptoms: the mood swings, the erratic impulsive behavior, weight loss, and then he developed a nasty rash on his face."

"So what did you do?"

"I don't mind telling you, I sweated my ass off for a couple of months. Dammit, I was losing weight over it myself. I was afraid he was going to screw up and kill someone—and then he did."

Gabe English looked up from his notes.

"I went straight to the top. I told the hospital CEO what I knew, what I'd seen, and what I suspected."

"What did he say?"

A look of utter disgust. "What do you think? He basically told me to shut up, that the patient would have died anyway. He reminded me that the Cabot had saved countless lives, and the excellent reputation of the hospital was due in part to his amazing skill.

"He did assure me that the hospital would take every precaution necessary to assure the health and well-being of all the people in it and those we served. He really emphasized the 'we.' No mistaking what he meant. Then he basically said that if I wanted to continue to be part of the team, I should continue with business as usual."

"That was it?"

Lincoln nodded. "That was it, and I sucked it up. I caved."

"What changed your mind?"

"It got to the point where I couldn't look myself in the eye. I had to do something. I had to stop what was going on. But I didn't get the chance. Somebody got there ahead of me."

Both detectives jerked to attention.

"What?"

He made a guttural noise that was halfway between a

choke and a snort. "Christ! Talk about a slip of the tongue. What I mean is, I had to speak up. Even if it did cost me my job...I just had to. And then somebody killed him. I didn't know what to do."

"Why are you talking to us now?"

"One of the problems is solved, Detectives. Jim Cabot is dead. But the hospital is still involved in a huge cover-up surrounding what he did and what he was doing. He was dealing drugs. They were covering that up too. It was not just a couple of bottles of pills here and there. It was big business."

Lincoln stopped to take a sip of his coffee. "Here's the thing. I think Jim Cabot was involved with the drug thing. I think he started using himself, and then I think maybe he started dealing on the side. He wouldn't be the first. It's easy for doctors to get pills. And then I think something went very, very wrong." Lincoln paused and dropped his voice. Wanda and Gabe leaned in closer.

"I grew up in a housing project right here in Boston. Single mom—the whole bit. I knew what was going on in the streets. We all did. Drugs. Everywhere. Guns and drugs. My mom did the best she could, but that wasn't much. She kinda gave up. It was a guy at the Boys and Girls Club who spotted me...and....well, I guess he saved my ass. He saw something in me."

He stopped and rubbed his eyes before continuing. "He got me a full ride to BU, pre-med. After that, I joined the Navy, and they sent me to med school. I did my twenty years, and here I am. Believe me, officers. I've seen it all. And I know a rotten mess when I see one, and I can't look away from this one any longer."

"It's none of my business, but what are you going to do now?" asked Gabe.

Lincoln threw up his hands. "I have to relocate. No

choice. I can't stay there. Not now. That's why I insisted on anonymity. If this gets out, I'll never find another job."

"You're good as far as we're concerned. This took courage. Thank you."

"I don't feel very brave. As long as I kept quiet about everything, I felt it made me one of them, and it was killing me inside."

"We all make choices. I think you made very good one."

"I hope so."

The meeting was over. Their barely touched coffee cups were cold on the table in front of them. Wanda walked up to the counter and paid the bill.

The three shook hands and went back out into the pale, cold December day. When they reached the edge of the sidewalk, Gabe reached out and touched Darnel Lincoln on the arm.

"Yeah?"

"You need to watch your back, Doctor. And if you ever need us, you call."

"Thanks, my man." He smiled, "And call me Darnel, okay?"

And then he was gone.

"Jesus H. Christ." Wanda shivered and fumbled in her pocket for her keys. "It's getting really cold out. They said we were in for a cold snap. I guess this is it. I think Lincoln's telling the truth. And if he is, it's pointed us in a whole new direction as far as the murder goes. The drug business is not on our patch, but I have no doubt that Boston's finest will be only too happy to hear about it. No names, of course."

"Man, oh, man is the shit gonna hit the fan in there."

Gabe responded with a doubtful look. "Maybe it will, and maybe it won't. Depends on who's in bed with who."

"You're joking," said Wanda.

"I only wish I was."

She nodded grimly. "I must be getting old. And please, don't answer that."

He held up his hands in mock defense. "I think that, before we do anything else, we go straight back to the station, call BPD, and tell them what we just learned. We can't sit on that."

She sighed. "What was that about time off on the weekend?"

"What's a weekend?"

She waved away the thought.

"Okay, call it whatever you want. Just stay warm, okay? It's gonna be cold as hell for the next couple of days, and we've got work to do."

"Wonderful," moaned Wanda. "Just ducky."

19

Out of the ICU and improving steadily on a regular medical unit, Emilio waited until the midday meal had been delivered and picked up. Nap time, they told him and encouraged him to try and sleep as much as he could so he could get his strength back. He smiled and nodded and asked if they would pull the curtain around his bed.

On the pretext of getting up to use the toilet, he pulled his clothes out of the locker and headed into the bathroom. Weak and dizzy, but so much better than when he'd first come in, he slowly took off the hospital johnny and pulled on his clothes. Then he rolled up his pants, put the johnny back on, draped a hospital-issue bathrobe over everything, and completed his exit outfit with a scrub-cap and a surgical face-mask. Thus attired, he made his way slowly out of the room and started down the hall, where in a moment of divine inspiration, he grabbed an orphaned IV pole, as much for balance as for cover, and shuffled into the elevator. He looked like any other patient going out for a forbidden cigarette. Nobody even looked up.

When he made it down to the first floor without incident, he ducked into the men's room, pulled off the hospital-issue clothing, wadded it up, and stuffed it into the wastebasket. He pushed the IV pole into the corner next to the toilet. After that, he put on his jacket and hat and wobbled out the door and across the street to the McDonald's.

He ordered as much food as he could afford, ate some of it, and took the rest with him. The day was bright, clear, and not particularly cold. The snow that had fallen earlier in the week was long gone, and while hitchhiking back to Loring by the Sea would take all the strength he could muster, at least he wouldn't freeze. He knew he could make it. He had no choice. In truth, he had to get out of there. If somebody did call the police, or the hospital reported him as undocumented, they would put him in jail and send him back to Brazil. He took a deep breath and started coughing. Mistake.

When the spasm passed, he took a much more moderate breath, walked to the edge of the sidewalk, and holding onto his food and a street sign with one hand, he held out his other hand and extended his thumb. Emilio prayed it wouldn't be too long before a kindly stranger would stop and offer a ride to a weak and shaky brown-skinned man.

That evening, in the undercroft of the church, Emilio lay in his bed and looked at his cell phone. He was still painfully weak and had a vicious and persistent cough. Until that abated, he knew he could not go back to work. Still, he was far better than he'd been on the day he'd collapsed upstairs. He'd called in to his boss and was assured his job was safe and to come back as soon as he could. The holidays were big business there, and it was all hands on deck, so the sooner the better. No pressure, of course.

Getting enough food to eat was soon going to be a problem. Not that he had much of an appetite right now, but the few things that he'd picked up in McDonald's were almost gone. Tonight, he'd creep upstairs and prowl around the church kitchen and see if there was anything that might have been left after one of the many events the church hosted.

Mostly, it was fruit juices and snack food: limp crackers, hard cheese, and orphaned grapes. One lucky day, he'd discovered an unopened pint of coffee cream and drank the whole thing on the spot and followed that with an enormous wedge of leftover chocolate birthday cake, a fork-full of which he'd shared with his mouse.

He took great care to leave no trace, other than the missing edibles. As a rule, churches did not count the cookies and the crackers that passed through the kitchen. But on that particular occasion, the midnight foraging did catch the attention of the church administrator, who himself had a sweet tooth, and truth be told, had his own eye on that particular piece of cake. Bennett suspected Olympia of the theft, but was too polite to say anything directly. Nonetheless, when it came to sugar…

Tomorrow was Sunday. Emilio knew he'd have to stay hidden for the entire day. The good news was that Sundays were always good for leftovers. Unless there was a wedding in the afternoon, once the service and the coffee hour were over and the kitchen cleaned up, everybody got out of the building and stayed out until Monday or sometimes even Tuesday. Emilio was hungry, and he was starting to feel stronger. Maybe, when the place emptied out tomorrow, he might just venture upstairs in the daylight and see what else he could find.

20

In Brookfield, the combined families of Andrea Riggs and her daughters, Frederick, Olympia, and the two cats, Thunderfoot and Cadeau, were becoming increasingly more comfortable with one another. The cats seemed particularly pleased with the additional attention and followed the girls around like two little meowing dogs.

It had been four days since her husband's murder, and now that the initial shock had worn off, the tears Andrea fought back fell more freely now and often without warning. The girls were working through it all in their own way. At times, they would follow their mother around, asking intense and weepy questions. In the next minute, they would pivot away and start playing with the cats or withdraw into a game on their ever-present tablets.

Because Andrea had agreed to stay on through the holidays, the two women were making tenuous Christmas plans. Olympia knew this would be a delicate operation—enough sparkle and glitz to make it feel like the real thing, but not too much. On one side was the effort to keep everything looking as normal as possible. On the other was the fact that a husband and father had just been killed, and there was an active murder investigation underway, an investigation directly involving the woman who was currently living with them, and an undocumented man who had reached out to the church for help and who was now missing.

Christmas is coming, the goose is getting fat, please to put a penny in the old man's hat. The bouncy, cheerful song kept running, however inappropriate to the situation, through Olympia's head. Damned earworms! She much preferred Britten's Ceremony of Carols, or even Jingle Bells, for God's sake, but she couldn't seem to tune in either of those at the moment.

Deal with the here and now, she chided herself. What will be will be.

Bing!

Andrea looked up at the clock on the shelf over the woodstove. "I thought that clock didn't work."

"It doesn't," said Frederick.

"It just binged."

"Possibly the heat from the stove, you know, expansion and contraction? But never mind. What we need to do right now is talk about getting a Christmas tree."

This brought both girls to bright-eyed attention.

"A real one? Daddy never let us have a real one. He said they made a mess."

Andrea bit her lip and looked away.

"Of course we'll get a real one. We'd never have anything else. Would we, Olympia?" Frederick beamed at the prospect. Perhaps, he was remembering when he and Olympia bought their own first tree.

Now the girls were literally bouncing up and down, their words tumbling over each other's. "A really, really, really big one? When can we go get it? Can we all pick it out? Can we all decorate it?"

A second contented *bing* issued from the old wooden clock. Frederick held up his teacup in the clock's direction and winked.

Andrea looked simultaneously amused and confused. "Is there something going on here that I should know about?" she asked with a half-curious smile.

"Later," said Olympia. "The clock came with the house, and now it can't keep its mouth shut. I think it thinks it owns the place."

This did nothing to clarify Andrea's growing confusion.

"Later." Olympia winked and tapped the side of her nose with her index finger.

"When can we get the tree?"

"I've got an idea. Why don't you three go out with Frederick tomorrow morning and get the tree while I'm at church? Then when I get back, we can spend the afternoon decorating it."

"Don't you want to help pick it out?"

"I do, but I like to be surprised too. You can surprise me this time. Make sure you get a really, really, really good one." She wagged a finger at them.

"A big, fat one."

Olympia winked at Frederick. They could do this. Then the phone rang.

"What now?" Frederick scowled and went for the phone while Olympia remained in her chair, looking worried.

"Oh, hi there, Jim. We weren't just talking about you, but we soon would have been had we continued, which we didn't because we were interrupted by your call."

Everybody in the room, including the cats, listened and tried to understand one side of a totally cryptic conversation. Frederick laughed, playing to his audience.

"No, no, dear boy. It's just that we were talking about Christmas, making plans you know, and this would eventually lead to our calling and confirming that you and Andrew would be joining us for Christmas dinner and staying the night. What say you?"

Olympia waved, made the thumb-and-baby-finger-phone signal, and pointed vigorously to herself.

"Hold on. I think my good lady wife doth wish a word with thee. Here, I'll put her on and let you two work out the details."

Olympia got out of her chair. "I'll take it in the office. Clerical stuff."

BOING-BOING-BOING, said the clock.

"Uh-oh," said Frederick.

"Will somebody please tell me what's going on with that clock?" said Andrea.

Olympia shut the door behind her and cranked up the heat a few notches. Her office was drafty, and the night was cold and getting colder.

"Hi, Jim. I'm glad you called. Things around the church seem to have gone to hell in a handbasket since I talked to you last. I need information, and I need advice, most likely in equal quantities."

After a bit of time and calendar juggling, the two friends agreed to meet the next morning at ten, after the commuter rush, at their favorite halfway spot in Weymouth. It was an authentic vintage train-car diner called the Krusty Krumpet. Despite the ridiculous name and the tacky, fifties-era, all-American décor, the food was great, plentiful, and cheap. Jim, the ultimate gourmet snob, had to be convinced the first time they went there, but the oven-baked, puffy Dutch-apple pancake had won the day.

"Tomorrow at ten, then?"

"Red booth on the end if I can get it."

DECEMBER 1865

Cold and clear today and our poor Lottie, who is quite unused to cold weather, wraps herself in layers and layers of shawls and stays near the fire whenever she can. She says little, and other than sometimes playing cat's cradle with the children, she keeps to herself. She is still so very frightened, and it is all I can do to keep her from running out of the room to hide when there is a knock at the door. I cannot bear to think of what she has endured and what pain and suffering has brought her to this sorry state. I am of the belief that, in the fullness of time, she will begin to trust us. I have seen little glimmers of it: a quick smile, the shy offer to help with some household task, or her willingness watch the children when we have need of being elsewhere.

This week, I heard her singing in the sitting room. Of course, she went silent and hung her head when she saw me. But I tapped my ear, then my lips, and then with two fingers, pulled my lips into a smile. I was rewarded with a modest smile, but a smile, it was. Since then, like a little rosebud, she has started to unfold and tell us her story.

More anon...LFW

21

O n Sunday afternoon, after the social hour, after the last cup and plate had been washed and the leftovers wrapped and stashed in the fridge, Olympia returned to her office. Rather than following fast on the tail of the last die-hard parishioner to drive out of the parking lot, Olympia often spent an hour or so with her feet propped on the bottom drawer, winding down and relaxing. This was a time when she reviewed the sermon, went over the notes she took during the coffee hour, and thought about the week ahead. She also thought with some pleasurable anticipation about the over-sized glass of wine that Frederick would have chilled and waiting for her when she returned to the house.

"Reverend?"

Olympia looked up to see the two detectives she'd met the night of the murder standing in the doorway. Behind them, Franklin Bowen hovered, looking darkly anxious. He huffed and sputtered about making appointments because the reverend was a busy woman, and they couldn't just...

Olympia hastily resumed a more upright position and leaned forward, elbows on her desk. "Come in, Detectives.

We've met before. Come in, and sit down where we can be warm and comfortable. It's getting really cold out there, isn't it?" She offered them her most engaging smile. "And while I'm delighted to have you here, I have the feeling this might not be a purely social call."

Wanda Licowski was the first to speak. "You're right, Reverend. I'm afraid this is business, the same unfortunate business that brought us together the other night." She stopped, looked around the room, and then up at the high molded ceiling. "Wow. You know, I've worked in this town for years and I've never been inside this church. It's beautiful. Lots of history too, I'm told."

"It's on the National Register," said Olympia.

"They laid the first stone in 1789." Franklin had managed to follow the two detectives into the office and once there, made no attempt to leave. This was more excitement he'd been witness to in years, and he wasn't about to miss a single minute of it. That, and a chance to expound on the illustrious history of the church was almost more than his stout heart could bear, but he was managing nicely.

Olympia indicated the seating area near the window. "Please, do sit down, everyone. Let's find out what brings you to our door."

The two detectives glanced simultaneously toward Franklin with giant question marks in their eyes.

"This is Franklin Bowen. He's the president of the congregation. Anything that involves the church and any kind of decision-making regarding the church would automatically involve him. So if it's all the same to you, I'd just as soon he stayed."

Franklin smiled, leaned back in his chair, and anchored in for the duration. In that moment, he swore total and complete allegiance to the lady interim minister. Neither of them knew how much that was going to involve.

Detective English opened the conversation. "Reverend Brown, we understand that on Thursday morning of this week, a man was taken ill here in this church and had to be transported by ambulance to South Coast General. Is that true?"

Olympia nodded. "Poor man. I don't know what made him think to come here, but I'm so glad he did. He was really sick."

"Did you know him before the event, Reverend? His name is Emilio Vieira. We learned that from the 911 call."

"He came to church from time to time on a Sunday, and even came to coffee hour once in a while. But did I know him before he took sick? Only to speak to. He was nice enough but not really very social."

"So you knew him?"

"I just told you, only to speak to. The day he collapsed, I went with him in the ambulance because he was alone. I asked him if there was someone we should call. He said he had no family here, and he lived alone. I went back and visited him the next day, and he was still sick, but he was definitely getting better. I planned to go again, but when I got there on Saturday, he wasn't there."

"So he'd been released by then?"

"I didn't say that. The people at the hospital just told me he was no longer a patient there. You know HIPPA laws. Even with my clerical collar on, they wouldn't tell me anything."

"Has he been in touch with you? Do you know where he is now?"

"No and no, but I wish he'd contact me."

"Why is that, Reverend?" asked Wanda.

"Clearly, the man is alone, and he needs help. Isn't that what churches and charitable people everywhere, churched or not, try to do? All year round, of course, but especially now, around Christmas? Feed the hungry, befriend the stranger? Wouldn't you say?" Olympia cocked her head and smiled at the man.

"Of course I agree, Reverend, and at the same time, I'm sure you are aware of what happened in this town earlier this week."

She shot him a dark look. "You and I both know what happened. That's why you came to my house, if you remember, and if you don't, I do."

"We are looking for a murderer, Reverend. We have to follow up on any information that comes in to us, and I mean anything. We've gotten several tips about a dark-skinned man, often seen riding a bicycle, who's been spotted around town and more than once right around here, near this church."

"Well, if it's the same man, and it probably is, I already told you, he's from Brazil. He comes to church once in a while, and he does ride a bike to get here. We all wish he'd spend more time with us. He's very polite."

"So you do know him."

Olympia slowly curled all of her fingers, one by one, into a tight little fist in her lap.

"I told you. I know him to speak to. I'd recognize him on the street, and I visited him in the hospital after he fell ill. Do we have a social or congregational relationship? No."

"What did you talk about when you visited him?"

She smiled and shook her head. "Sorry. Pastoral confidence."

Undaunted, Wanda continued. "Do you have any idea where he might be now? We'd like to talk to him."

"I honestly and truly do not, and I already told you that." She held up two fingers in a Boy Scout salute. "Scouts' honor."

"If you find out, will you tell us?"

"Only if he gives me permission."

"But…"

"I understand duty to inform, Detective. I understand that if I hear something in clerical confidence that could result in direct harm to the person telling me or to another person, I am obliged to break that confidence and alert someone who can help. I give you my word. If I feel it is warranted, I will absolutely perform that duty. But a church is supposed to be a sanctuary—a safe haven. As a minister, it is my duty and privilege to honor and protect that status." She paused. "And as a citizen, it is my duty to obey the law. The trouble is, sometimes, the two conflict. I give you my word, I'll do what I can. Now, is there anything else I can help you with?"

The two detectives got the unmistakable hint and rose to their feet.

"May we call on you again if we have more questions?"

"Of course."

Wanda held out a card. "Please take this, and if you hear of anything or think of anything you think might be of help, please call me. Okay?"

"Of course."

When the two detectives were well and truly gone, Franklin Bowen stood and held out his hand to Olympia.

"I wish I had a movie of that. You were unflappable."

"Thanks, Franklin. We live in interesting times, wouldn't you say?"

"I say you should go home and put your feet back up. You've had quite a day."

LATER, Detectives English and Licowski were back at the station comparing notes and asking questions.

English slipped several papers into a manila folder and set

it on his desk. "She's not just a pretty face, that minister-woman. She is one tough lady. You have to admire her."

"I do, but don't you think that it's a curious coincidence that the widow of the deceased, possibly a person of interest, came to the church in need of help and is now living at her house?" She held up one finger then added a second. "And the stranger on the bicycle, the one reported to have been seen in or near the neighborhood of the murder chose that same church to collapse in and has now conveniently disappeared. Both have connections to the minister of the big, white church in the center of town."

"Do you think it's just a random coincidence?"

"I don't believe in coincidence, and in this business, neither should you."

Gabe chuckled. "Just checking to see if you're awake, sister."

"Trust me. I'm awake, and I'm not liking what I'm seeing."

"And what are you seeing?"

"Major drug dealing out of a Boston hospital with possible connections to a local doctor. Not pretty, but hardly news. Money, greed, and addiction have no bounds and make no class distinctions. A prominent doctor, possibly, highly likely even, connected in some way to the drug issue, gets murdered in his own backyard. Wife of victim just happens to leave him the day before. People in town report seeing a dark-skinned stranger on a bicycle and start asking questions."

Gabe picked up the thread of the conversation. "A stranger who rides a bike and who has been known to come to the church on a Sunday. Is it the same man, we ask? Or is it another dark-skinned stranger also on a bicycle who just happens to be in town for that one night in pricey, lily-white, exclusive Loring by the Sea where bad things only happen on television?"

"Too many parallels. Too many connections and not enough hard information about where they intersect."

"Hold on a minute," said Wanda. "Think about this. If the victim was involved in the drug trade, it could be he screwed up big time, and they neutralized him. The drug business is usually linked to organized crime and professional hit men. That's not news either. Maybe he got greedy, tried to deal on his own, or he didn't deliver the goods, or he said the wrong thing to the wrong person, and they came after him. I don't really think this is a case of domestic violence. We now know the man was shot with a Glock Four. It's a popular street gun, high powered and deadly."

"The kind of gun a professional hit man would use."

Gabe nodded. "Another scenario is abused wifey talked to somebody who talked to somebody who knew somebody who knew how to get hold of a professional hit man...and she hired him."

"A dark-skinned man who gets around on a bicycle?"

"The bicycle part doesn't fit."

"What do you mean?"

"Professional killers drive cars. Or so I'm told. It's December. It's freezing out. You really think a killer is going to take a bike, shoot a guy in his backyard, and pedal away down the street?"

"Yeah. But there still could be a connection. We have to find the guy."

"So let's say we do find him, and we learn there's no connection to the murder. But what if he's innocent of the murder, but he's an illegal? She said he's Brazilian. If he's undocumented and he's living here, he's breaking the law. There're a lot of them around, living undercover....usually working shit jobs. What do we do then?"

"That doesn't make him a real criminal."

"No, but if he's here without a visa or a work permit, it makes him scared and therefore vulnerable to manipulation."

"Makes him open to getting money that won't be detected or being bribed or blackmailed?"

Gabe looked doubtful. "I say we have another chat with the grieving widow."

Wanda shook her head and held up her hands in surrender. "Tomorrow, Gabe. I'm totally thunk out. I'm going home."

22

W hen Olympia dragged herself through the door late that afternoon, all she wanted to do was sit down with that glass of wine she knew had her name on it. But this was not to be, at least, not immediately. First of all, she was absolutely freezing. The predicted cold snap had arrived on schedule, and it was not pleasant. The trees outside, stiffened by the cold, clattered when the wind stirred their branches. Even walking the short distance from her van to the back door made breathing difficult. The cats didn't even come near the back door when she opened it, but two bouncing, bright-eyed little girls did the honors.

"We got it."

"Come see."

"It's huge."

"It's sticky."

"Frederick had to cut the top off."

"The cats are trying to climb it."

"Can we start decorating now? Mummy said we had to wait until you got home."

"Sure." Olympia forced a toothy smile.

"Would you like a cup of tea first, my love?" asked Frederick. "Something to warm you up?"

"Sure," repeated Olympia. "I can't think of anything I'd like better."

"I'll wager you can," said Frederick. "But for the moment, it's good ole Rosie-Lee, the English cure for everything from a broken heart to…"

"Rosie-Lee?" asked Andrea who'd followed the girls into the kitchen.

"It's a long story, but I'll tell that story and the clock story after we decorate the tree and I've had a glass of wine."

It was ridiculous to suggest supper, but she did so anyway and was met with a jumbled chorus of, "later, after we finish the tree, I'm not hungry."

Olympia took that as a no and followed the squealing girls into the sitting room. There, a huge, fat, naked Christmas tree stood in the corner, well away from the woodstove, with its prickly arms outstretched, waiting to be adorned.

While they'd waited for Olympia to come home, the twins had set up shop at the kitchen table, cutting out paper stars and snowflakes and pasting up endless paper chains. Andrea appeared to be holding up, but from time to time, Olympia caught her biting her lip and staring off into space. Olympia kept an eye on her but said nothing. Considering the circumstances, the woman was doing pretty damned well.

By seven in the evening, the tree was resplendent and twinkling merrily in its appointed corner. The scent was heavenly. The cats had already shredded a paper star and the end of one of the paper chains, but those had been quickly repaired and re-hung.

A Sunday night supper of grilled cheese sandwiches, canned tomato soup, instant mac and cheese, and store-bought cookies completed the day, and they all sat, their plates in their laps, admiring the results of their creative efforts.

It took a while to get the girls wound down enough to go to bed, but eventually, the deed was done, and three weary grownups sat, each lost in his or her own thoughts in an easy silence around the fire. Christmas is a time for remembering, and the memories are always mixed—happy times, painful times, times of loss, and times of wonder and great joy.

Bing!

Andrea looked up from her cup of cocoa. "You were going to tell me the story of the clock."

"No time like the present." Olympia pulled herself up out of her own tangle of thoughts and pointed to the old clock. "She came with the house, and by now, we've come to think of her as one of the family."

Andrea did not look in the least bit enlightened.

Olympia chuckled. "It's all part of the fun. Do you believe in ghosts?"

"Does that make a difference?"

"Oh, Olympia, do get on with it, will you?"

Bing!

"See, even she's getting impatient."

Frederick and Olympia had played out this little scene more than once, and each time, they added something new and enjoyed it that much more.

"Okay," said Olympia. "The truth, the whole truth, and nothing but the truth. Ready or not."

Taking turns and sometimes even finishing one another's sentences, Frederick and Olympia told Andrea that they believed that the clock held the spirit of Miss Leanna Faith Winslow. She was, they explained, the last descendent of Mayflower passenger Otis Winslow, who built the house they now sat in. Furthermore, they explained that when Miss Winslow wanted to communicate with them, she did it though the clock.

Andrea was looking more skeptical by the minute.

"No, really," said Olympia. "It's true. You'll get used to it. We did."

Bing!

"Okay, what did she just say?" asked Andrea.

"She likes you, and she's happy we're here together."

"All that from one little bing?"

"She's a woman of few words," quipped Frederick. "Say, why don't you show Andrea Leanna's diary while I go make myself a cup of Rosie-Lee. That might help."

"Good idea, Frederick. Make me one too, will you?"

"And…" said a smiling Andrea. "You were also going to tell me about Rosie-Lee. I suppose that's the name of another spirit who lives here."

"It's Cockney rhyming slang for cup of tea," said Frederick. "Everybody knows that. Now, do you want one?"

"I've still got my cocoa, thanks."

Olympia reached out and patted Andrea on the arm. "I don't care how many time he tries to explain rhyming slang to me, I still don't really get it. But by now, I do know about Rosie-Lee."

Frederick returned with their teacups, put another log on the fire, and scooped up a cat. If a man hadn't been murdered earlier that week, and the sweet little family that was staying with him hadn't been there because of the actions of that man, everything would have seemed so very lovely and normal.

But it wasn't, and they all knew it.

Still, in that room, on that night, there was enough comfort and joy to go around. They knew that, too, but to speak of it would have broken the spell, and none of them wanted that.

THAT SAME NIGHT, in the sub-basement of the church,

Emilio was feeling better but the air around him was getting colder and colder. Because he was underground, he knew he wouldn't freeze, but something was wrong. Different. He realized he couldn't hear the hiss and thrum of the big, old furnace that heated the building and the crawl space where he slept at night and where he was now hiding from the police. What would happen now? What could he do? He didn't know anything about furnaces. Was there someone he could call? Should he call the reverend? She'd given him her number. Would the pipes freeze?

He'd heard the restaurant manager talking about that happening when the weather got really cold. But if he called someone, would they trace the call and find him? He finally decided he should call the reverend. But then what? What would he say? She would be sure to ask him how come he knew the furnace wasn't working. Hmmm, maybe he'd better not.

Emilio pulled up another blanket and drank some water. He was worried about what would happen if he got too cold. What if the pipes did freeze and broke and the building flooded? Would he have to find a new place to sleep? Then he remembered something else his boss had said about winters in New England. When it got really cold, he said, they always left the water dripping so the pipes wouldn't freeze.

With a low groan, Emilio dragged himself out of his rumpled cocoon and went out into the newer part of the building. By now, he knew where all the sinks and the faucets were located, so it was just a question of opening them slightly and letting them drip. And as long as he was up and out of his cave, he might as well have a look around the kitchen and see if there might be anything left there for him to eat.

23

On Monday mornings, traffic in and out of Boston was always more hectic than on other days. Thus, meeting at ten, after the big rush, gave Olympia and Jim a little extra running room and a much more relaxing drive.

The Krump, as the regulars affectionately called it, was an unvarnished local treasure, and they planned to keep it that way. It was word-of-mouth advertising only, and still, the place was always humming. It boasted regular menu items such as meatloaf Thursdays, pot roast Mondays, and an all-you-can-eat fish fry on Fridays. What it lacked in elegance, it made up in quantity, quality, and comical names for their dishes.

It took a while for Olympia to make them understand that, as a strict vegetarian, even fish was not an option. But once that hurdle was cleared, she enjoyed some of the best omelets, basil pasta, and fried mushrooms this side of the Charles River. That morning she'd ordered "The All-American Popeye," a spinach, tomato, and Swiss cheese omelet. She was in heaven. Jim was blissing out on the "Never-Netherland," their signature delight, a Dutch Apple pancake.

As they made their way through the mountain of food on

the table— Olympia had already asked for a doggie-box—she gave Jim the abbreviated version of the drama unfolding on both the work and home fronts. She concluded with the upsetting news that Emilio had vanished, and she had no idea where he was or what the state of his health was—and that the widow of the victim and her children would stay with her and Frederick through Christmas.

"Then what?" Jim cut his bacon into squares.

"To be continued, I guess. I don't know. She doesn't have to stay with my friend Evelyn Hightower in Plymouth now. But she doesn't want to go back to the house in Loring either. I can't say as I blame her on that score. Eventually, the kids are going to have to go back to school. But she can only do one thing at a time."

Jim nodded. He never spoke with his mouth full.

"I'm kind of in limbo here. The police are asking questions about Andrea, and they're also questions about Emilio. They didn't say it directly, but I gather they are both considered to be persons of interest."

"Next of kin is always the first place they start," said Jim. "It's understandable, particularly where there's evidence of domestic violence. And I'm assuming there is."

"Oh, there was evidence, all right. He pulled a chunk of hair right out of her head. Poor thing. She looked like a frightened animal when she walked into my office with those sweet, little kids. I wonder what else they've witnessed."

"Probably more than she knows or wants to think about. Kids don't miss much. But what about Emilio? Where does he fit into all of this?"

"The police are looking for him. After the murder they got calls about a stranger who had been seen riding around town on a bicycle. Merry F-ing Christmas! Go get the stranger," she spat.

"They're scared, Olympia."

"I get it, but dammit, why do people act like that?"

"Fear of the other. It's tribal. It's in our DNA." Jim sectioned his pancake into triangles.

"I thought we'd made a little bit of progress since then."

"Not when confronted with fear. That's when all our animal instincts kick in."

"My cats are better than that."

He shook his head. "No, not if they're panicked, they're not. And speaking of cats, you should see Sebastien, your undocumented French import. He is gorgeous, and he totally rules the house. Andrew is besotted with him. He is the master. We are the slaves."

Olympia chuckled. "Father James Sawicki, never in my born days did I ever think I'd hear you go all gushy over a cat. You've changed more than your religious affiliation, my boy."

"I've always liked animals, Olympia. I've just never had the chance to have one of my own. Thank you for that. But let's get back to Emilio. You say he's disappeared."

"I'll amend that. I don't know where he is. He did ask me to call his boss at the restaurant and tell him what was going on and to please save his job."

"And did you?"

"Of course."

"If he's planning to go back to work, that means he's probably in the vicinity. The question is where?"

Olympia shrugged. "No idea, and I can't do anything about that. I can only hope he'll contact me. I can't believe I didn't ask for his number, but I didn't. We had a good talk in the hospital. I think I gained his trust. He showed me a picture of his baby."

"Baby?"

"It's so sad. His wife died in childbirth. His mother and sisters are taking care of his daughter. He's been working locally for almost a year. He's trying to get enough money to bring them all here."

"And he overstayed his visa."

Olympia nodded. "On that subject, did you find out anything from your BPD friend, Jerry O'Brien, about immigration law and where we can get help for undocumented people? If Emilio does turn up, and I'm inclined to think he will, I want to have something to tell him. I want to give him something to hope for and hold on to. There has to be something."

"Don't ever change, Olympia."

"Couldn't if I tried."

Jim dabbed at his mouth, set his utensils on the side of the plate, and topped up his coffee.

"Okay, I saw Jerry, and he gave me a couple of names and numbers you can look into, immigration lawyers, help and hotlines. It's really tricky. These people stay under the radar, even those who want to help. Your friend made a big mistake letting the visa lapse. But if his record is clean, we might be able to do something. At the very worst, he might have to leave and then reapply to come back, but that's not the end of the world, especially if we can find people to sponsor him."

Olympia raised her hand. "You know I will. Who knows, maybe I can even get the church to take it on as a social action/social justice project."

Jim favored her with his well-practiced, skeptical, over-the-glasses lengthy stare. "You're the optimist, and I'm the realist, but I do think that might be pushing the miracle concept a bit too far."

"But…"

"Look, Olympia. You don't even know where he is right now. He may or may not come back to the church. I suppose you can call the restaurant and see if he's turned up, but don't be surprised if they won't tell you. These people know how to hide, and they depend on their friends to cover for them, but it's no way to live."

"I want to help him, Jim."

"I know you do, and now we've got some options. All we have to do is find him so we can tell him."

"He's got options if the police don't pick him up and charge him with murder."

"You never make it easy for yourself, do you, Olympia? Come on, girlfriend. Time to get moving."

"Hold on, one more thing. You and Andrew *are* going to come and spend Christmas day and night with us." It was not a question.

"Already on the calendar. He's going to love it. He comes from a big family, but it's been years since he's been with them. They pretty much disowned him when he came out. It's been lonely for him, and it would have been for me too if you hadn't taken me in when you did."

Olympia looked deeply into the eyes of her best friend. "God, that seems a lifetime ago, doesn't it, Jim? Lots of water under that bridge, my friend."

He reached across the table for her hand and gave it a squeeze. "Damn sure is, my friend."

WHILE OLYMPIA and Jim were catching up and comparing notes at the Krump, all hell was breaking loose at the First Parish Church of Loring by the Sea. Gordon Bennett had come in at his appointed time and was surprised to find the place igloo-cold. He checked the thermostat, thinking that someone, possibly Olympia, might have inadvertently turned it off when she left. They always left it set for 60, but it read 42 degrees. Not good. No wonder he felt cold. He pushed up the arrow on the wall gauge to 72 and heard nothing—no predictable click and hum of the furnace coming on. Gordy didn't like building emergencies.

"Oh, my God, the pipes." He knew this was an old building, and the insulation was far from perfect. He knew what broken pipes could do to a place. He wasted no time in going into the men's bathroom to look for leaks or puddles. He was amazed and slightly spooked to find the taps had been opened, and water dripped freely into the sink. He found the same thing in the upstairs ladies' room, the kitchen sink, and in the children's teeny-toilet bathroom in the basement.

Did the church have a guardian angel whose duty it was to look after the plumbing? He laughed at his own joke, more because he was nervous than his mild attempt at humor. How —or more likely, who—had turned on the pipes? He knew the place was rumored to have one or two restless souls floating about but preferred not to dwell on the subject. Bennett was a self-confessed scaredy-cat when it came to anything out of his comfort zone.

Then he really did laugh, this time, in blessed relief. Of course, it had to have been Franklin. Who else? He had a key, and he was obsessed with the welfare and preservation of the building. Whew!

As if on cue, the man himself walked into the office.

"Morning, Gordy. I just came in to check on things. The temperature really dropped last night. I just hope nothing froze. I thought about coming over here last night and check-ing, but I fell asleep. I must be getting old. Hey, it's like ice in here. You forget to turn up the heat?" He laughed.

Gordy, wide-eyed, slowly shook his head. "You mean, you didn't come over here last night and turn on the faucets? Oh, and I think the furnace broke. I tried to turn it on when I came in, and nothing happened."

"Did you go downstairs and look?"

The administrator shook his head. "Wouldn't have done any good if I had. I don't know the first thing about plumbing and heating. Give me a desk and a computer any day. I was about to call you." What the man didn't say was that you couldn't have paid him to go into the dark and mouse-and-spider-filled nooks and crannies of that place. No way.

Franklin put his hands on his hips. "Well, now that I'm here, I'll go look, but if you say it won't come on, it's probably done for. Perfect timing, wouldn't you say? Christmas coming and all. We've been patching it up for years. Damn thing's older than dirt. Should have replaced it years ago. God knows I wanted to, but nobody listens, do they?" He harrumphed and beckoned to Bennett to follow him.

The last place he wanted to go was down into the old part of the church, but with Franklin right there, he really had no choice.

"Wait a minute," said Gordy, "You didn't come in here last night and turn the water on in the sinks?"

"I told you I didn't. What are you getting at?"

Gordy shivered. "Somebody did."

"Really?" Franklin Bowen simply nodded while making a mental note to have a chat with Olympia about Bennett's fitness for the job. "No point wasting time. Let's do it."

"Uh, why don't you go check on the furnace, and I'll... stay up here by the phone? I can start looking up plumbers."

Bowen gave up. "We have a plumber. His name is in the file labeled Contractors. And while you're at it, you might as well call Reverend Olympia, and let her know what's happening. Not that she can do anything. Buildings and grounds are in charge of that. But it's good to be courteous."

"Is she coming in this morning?"

"I don't know. She usually takes Mondays off. Sunday's her big day, and she needs to rest up. No need for her to freeze in here. If you do get her, tell her not to come in. You stay here. I'll be right back."

Bennett was only too happy to do as he had been told and breathed a noisy sigh of relief as Franklin left the office and started down the stairs.

❄

EMILIO HEARD the approaching footsteps and froze. He hadn't planned to still be there, but it was too late now. After a few restless hours of not sleeping, he'd fallen into a deep, healing sleep. In his exhaustion, he'd forgotten to turn off his phone, and while he slept, it had died, and there was no alarm to awaken him. Now, he was trapped. Please, God, he prayed, don't let me cough. I can always pee in a bottle. Anything else will have to wait.

THE FURNACE WAS a giant octopus of a thing. With all of its ducts and pipes and knobs and dials, it sat, glowering in silence, in the outer section of the old, stone cellar. It even smelled mean. Franklin Bowen circled it, not really knowing what he was looking for. He did know to check the fuel gauge. It read three-quarters full. Bad. He knew about the reset button. He pushed it. Nothing. Very big bad. No point wasting any more time. It was time to call in the professionals. With luck, and he would emphasize that it was an emergency, it might be possible to get someone there within the hour.

IN HIS HIDEY-HOLE, Emilio heard the muttering of someone prowling around in the cellar not six feet from where he was crouched. Hardly daring to breathe, lest he might start coughing, he leaned against the removable panel in what only could be described as heart-pounding, clammy-palmed, teeth-chattering, abdominal-cramping terror. He stared into the surrounding darkness and prayed that no one would ever think of looking into the almost-forgotten crawl space under the stairs.

24

On impulse, Father Jim decided to pay a second visit in three days to his friend Jerry O'Brien. Jim didn't do too many things on impulse. He preferred an ordered life, knowing full well that this was not always possible.

He enjoyed his meetings with Jerry. It gave them both a chance to reminisce about their Polish-Irish childhood memories of a childhood in a working-class neighborhood of double- and triple-decker homes in a corner of the city that was home to mostly first-generation immigrants trying to gain a foothold in the land of opportunity. A city that joked cruelly about dumb Polaks—and handwritten signs that read, "No Irish need apply," were commonplace in store windows and outside factories. One group at the bottom of the socioeconomic ladder vied with the other for anything resembling respect. In this setting, Jim and Jerry had swum against the tide of immigrant nationalism and become fast friends.

Their friendship had withstood the risk and fear of Jim's coming out of the closet. It had withstood the disgrace of Irish Catholic Jerry's divorce from his first-generation Italian wife and refusing to pay the church for an annulment so he could marry a Swedish Protestant. They were buds.

"Father Jim, me boy. And what is that brings yer back to me door so sudden-like?" Jerry often affected a phony Irish accent in his old friend's company because it never failed to make him laugh. This was no exception.

"I was driving by, saw your car, and took a chance you might have a few minutes."

"Then we're both in luck. Sit down, and take a load off your mind. Confession, is it?"

Jim smiled and mouthed the word asshole at his old friend. "Business. Same stuff I called you about the other day."

The joking banter and virtual sucker- punching vanished. "What's up? They get the guy, and your minister lady-friend needs help?"

"No. The Brazilian guy seems to have dropped off the radar for the moment. It's something else."

"Mmmm?"

"What do you know about that Boston doctor, cardiologist I think, who was shot outside his home in Loring by the Sea?"

"Jesus, Jim, you don't fool around. How the hell did you get wind of that one? Oh, never mind, It's your minister friend again, isn't it? Don't tell me she's mixed up in that too. Good God in heaven, that woman gets around. She's as bad as you are."

Jim nodded. "She's the minister in one of the churches in the town where it happened. His widow and two children are staying at her house."

Jerry leaned back in his squeaky desk chair and crossed his arms over a middle-aged belly. "So tell me…everything."

When Jim finished, Jerry asked, "Confessional silence, right?"

Jim nodded.

"For the last two years, BPD and the drug and alcohol investigation people have been working undercover on cracking a mega opioid operation they think is operating out of one or more of the Boston hospitals. It's deeply connected to organized crime and millions, if not billions, of dark money. We think the victim, Dr. James Cabot, old Boston name and old Boston money, was deeply involved, screwed up, and got himself neutralized. The thing is, the case is much bigger than the murder. Dismissive as it sounds, the murder of one operator is little more than collateral damage in something like this. And it spirals out. The point is, the investigation involves about five different agencies—drug and alcohol, state police, medical ethics, money laundering…you name it. The one thing they don't want to get out is that this investigation is going on at all."

"I don't understand," said Jim. "Isn't that what you do want to do? Get it out there. Rip the cover off. Expose it to light and then grab the cockroaches as they run for cover."

"Yes, indeed, my man. But not yet. When this does hit the fan, and it will, there's a lot of heads gonna roll. If there's a leak ahead of time, it could derail the whole thing. Cabot's getting himself killed will, of course, start an investigation. If in the course of that investigation, the extent of his drug dealing comes out, the river-rats will run to ground, and we won't catch them. They'll hide out for a few months and then set up shop somewhere else and go right on dealing…and killing. These dirtbags are the scum of the scum, and from what I hear, we're too close now to let them get away."

Jim looked perplexed. "What should I tell Olympia to do? She's involved, all right. She's got the victim's widow living with her. And the missing Brazilian, Emilio, who is now a person of interest in the murder, has turned up at her church on more than one occasion. He's probably the convenient stranger seen biking around town who's so easy and convenient for everyone to suspect. You know, when in doubt, blame the stranger."

Jerry shook his head. "She's in dangerous waters. If they think she knows something, the killer could make a return visit. The widow lady should get herself a lawyer and stay well out of the public view. What I'm saying is, the widow could become collateral damage as well. And trust me. They will be looking for her. Under no circumstances should she go back to the house. They'll be watching it."

"They who?"

"The good guys and the bad guys; the cops…and the robbers. Everybody's got skin in this game. Tell Olympia to keep her doors locked. She shouldn't be at risk unless they find out where the widow is staying."

Jim rubbed his head. He was trying to process all that he'd just heard.

"Merry Christmas!" It was all he could think of to say.

"You got that right. And murderers and drug-dealers do not take holidays. In fact, holidays can be a convenient distraction."

"I don't get it."

"People let down their guard during a holiday season—all that 'peace on earth and good will toward men stuff' on the radio and in the air. The field is open. I mean, like, who's gonna rob a bank or kill someone on Christmas Eve?"

"Jesus," said Jim.

"Him too," said his old friend.

OUTSIDE THE KRUMP, Olympia was pulling out of the parking lot when her phone rang. She prudently drove straight back into her space before answering. She knew the dangers of distracted driving and didn't take chances. It was the church number.

"Hello, this is Reverend Olympia."

"Hey, Reverend, this is Gordy Bennett over at the church. We've got a problem here." Olympia's heart lurched under her winter jacket. A death, a break-in, a fire?

"The furnace quit, and the place is like an icebox. Franklin Bowen is here with the buildings and grounds people. They're going around plugging in little space heaters near the pipes to keep 'em from freezing, and we got a heating guy on his way over right now. Franklin says there's nothing you can do, so you should not come in just so you can sit and freeze."

"Oh, gosh, that's not good. Thank you for letting me know. Say, is Franklin still there? Could you put him on, please?"

A mumbled pause.

"Hi, Franklin. Talk about perfect timing. Well, I suppose it could have been worse. Better than on December twenty-fourth, in time for the kids' Christmas pageant. We'd have little snow angels singing from on high."

Franklin was not amused. "I'm no expert, Reverend, but by the looks of it, I'd say we have to get a new furnace and pronto. Not exactly the best Christmas present I can think of. And because of the season, we're going to have to take what we can get. No time for bargain hunting, I'm afraid…and there goes the budget."

Olympia made a number of soothing and sympathetic sounds before speaking actual words. "Good heavens. But what I hear you saying is we have the resources. It's just seriously inconvenient."

"That's about right, Reverend." He groaned responsibly.

"Okay then, if you're sure I can't be of any help, I will do as you suggest and head back home. There's plenty I can do from there. Just call in from time to time, will you, and let me know how things are progressing. And if any calls come in for me, please tell them to call me at home."

Olympia pocketed her phone and started toward the main road. This time, she turned left instead of right and made straight for the nearest shopping center. She loathed shopping centers, but at Christmas time, there was no way of avoiding them if you still had last-minute shopping to accomplish. She hated the mind-numbing commercialization of Christmas, but there was little she could do about that either. She was not anti-Christmas. Just the opposite. She LOVED Christmas: the carols, the lights, the decorations, the story of the miracle of birth, even if Jesus was likely born in April. Who cared? She truly enjoyed all of it. It was the incessant media pressure to be picture-book perfect and spend money you don't have to keep up with everyone else that troubled her. Where was the balance point? Could there ever be one? This had been the subject of more than one of her Christmas sermons.

Olympia pulled into the convoluted parking lot of one of the smaller shopping sites and found a spot. She did most of her shopping in thrift shops, discount department stores, craft shops, church fairs, and online. She'd already stashed away things for Frederick and Jim, for her two sons and their significant others, and had mailed off the gifts intended for her oldest child, Laura, her wife Gerry, and her beloved only grandchild. All she needed was a few token, non-obligatory surprises for Andrea and the girls to put under the tree. And while she was at it, something for Andrew, Jim's significant other.

She opened the car door and slid off the high seat down to the pavement. She was assaulted on all sides by the unbelievable cold and the sound of scratchy loudspeakers blaring, "Joy to the World! The Lord is come!" nonstop all the way to grandmother's house and back. She winced, covered her mouth and nose against the cold, and made a dash for the nearest entrance.

Her personal comfort and joy was the thought of getting home early and hanging out with cats and her newly reconfigured family. Temporary though it was, the thought of kids and old-fashioned Christmas magic warmed the cockles of her weary, fifty-something-year-old heart and released the hopeful little kid who lived within her.

5 DECEMBER, *1865*

Where has the time gone? It has been weeks since I took pen in hand and picked up this precious volume, this keeper of my thoughts. We have come to Brookfields for Christmas, and the weather is lovely. It is cold and clear, but high thin clouds are sliding in overhead, and this can only mean snow.

Susan and I and the children are delighted at the prospect, but poor Lottie is still perishing from the cold. She is a brave woman and doing her best to adjust to the climate, but I know she suffers. Still, as she is quick to tell us, it is better to be cold and free than warm and in bondage. Poor woman. She has seen so much in her not so many years, and with each passing day, we learn more of her tragic tale and her amazing courage. Hearing such a sad story in the words of a woman who has lived through it only strengthens my own resolve—and Susan's as well—to continue our abolitionist work. Nathan continues to improve. He wonders if having a dog might be helpful. I think I shall need to consult with the cat.

More anon…LFW

25

On Tuesday, less than a week before Christmas, in a closed conference room at BPD headquarters, Lieutenant Beth McAdams, the woman in charge of the Code Blue drug ring investigation, addressed the two people in the room. "Right, I'll get the warrant. I want you two to do a complete search of Cabot's house. We know the guy was OCD. We know he kept meticulous records of every medical procedure he ever performed. We've been over every millimeter of his office and his car, and so far, nada. There's a stash and records somewhere, and I'll lay money that the dry-eyed widow knows one hell of a lot more than she's telling us. I want you to bring her in again."

"Are you sure you want to do that?"

"What do you mean?" A nasty scowl.

"I mean, on the off chance she really doesn't know anything about hubby's little side job, isn't this gonna be like pouring salt into the wound?"

"Jesus. Who the hell are you kidding? Give me a break, will you? I'd be more than surprised if she doesn't already know or at least have some sort of idea that all was not as it appeared. On the other hand, there are people who manage to lead a double life, and they go on for years without being discovered. So you wanna know what I'm doing for the holidays? I'm chasing scumbags and dirt-balls. That's what I'm doing."

McAdams choked out a bitter laugh and dismissed the investigating detectives. "You go have yourselves a merry little Christmas, okay? Druggies don't take holidays. Cops don't either."

"Bah," said one of the detectives.

"Humbug," said the other.

"Ten-four," said McAdams.

HEAT OR NO HEAT, after a day of working from home, Olympia decided she needed to go in to work on Wednesday even if she didn't stay very long. It was important to be a caring presence in times of trouble. Earlier that morning, she'd checked in with Franklin Bowen and learned that they'd managed, using a number of space heaters and fans, to get the allover building temperature into the forties and the church offices up to a balmy sixty-two. The church proper, the worship space, because there were no water pipes anywhere near, was closed off and left to its own devices. He told her they'd already ordered a new furnace and that demolition and removal of the old one would start that day. It was the goal of all concerned to have the new one installed and running by the end of the week—all done and dusted and good to go for Christmas services.

Ever prudent and not a little mindful of her own comfort, Olympia put a portable heater and an extra sweater in the back of the van. Then she pushed her portable coffee cup into its holder, belted up, and set off. Driving time was her thinking time, and with two Christmas-crazy six-year-olds and a mother who came in and out of an altered grief-state, this was some blessed alone time. Time to review what was happening under her own roof. All in all, she thought between sips of coffee and keeping a watchful eye on the road ahead, Andrea was doing magnificently. By now, the kids understood something had happened to them all that changed everything. Olympia didn't think they fully comprehended the enormity of the changes, but she also knew that kids are amazingly resilient.

She was confident, knowing she'd done all she could for them for the time being. Everything would change after the start of the New Year, when the kids would have to go back to school, and Andrea would have to decide where that was going to be. She'd said nothing about her thoughts on that subject as yet.

On a more cheerful and predictable note, Jim and Andrew were coming for Christmas dinner and would likely stay the night. Olympia blessed her own foresight in getting a queen-sized sleep sofa for her office. She wondered how Andrea would handle the reality of two men, declared partners now, spending the night in the house. She would bring that up tonight when she got home.

Her boys would not be there for Christmas but would join them on Boxing Day, and ever-so-British Frederick would get to explain, once again, the holiday that was not a holy day but an English Victorian tradition, created by the landed gentry. It was a way to favor the servants and the lesser born with boxes of holiday leftovers as well a time to give small monetary tokens of appreciation to the tradespeople—the delivery men, the postman, the butcher, and the rubbish collectors. So very gratuitous.

Back to the shopping list, Olympia ticked off the gift categories on her chilly fingers. Had she missed anyone? No. Then she thought of Emilio, and her shoulders dropped in dismay. Where was he? Where would he be on Christmas Eve and Christmas Day? She added him to the list and decided to call in to the restaurant again and ask if they'd heard from him. And if they had, would they tell her? Maybe she should go over and see the manager herself without calling ahead. The surprise factor produced interesting results. She'd used it once or twice before.

Olympia rounded the corner on Main Street and saw the stately white church building directly ahead of her, firmly and centrally ensconced on the town green. There was a lot of history in that place—American colonial history, revolutionary history, civil and world wars one and two history, and history yet to be made. Even as an interim, a temporary minister of that church, she too would be part of that history and wondered what kind of mark she would leave on those time-honored walls.

SHE REMEMBERED Jim suggesting the church might want to consider taking on Emilio's plight as a social justice initiative. She thought about it a second time. First, she had to find the man. What happened after that would be anyone's guess. *Get yourself into the office first, Olympia, and check on the progress of the new furnace. Without heat, you don't have services.* The tune and the words of the carol, "In the bleak midwinter, frosty wind made moan," came to mind. Yup, she nodded to an unseen presence, 'tis the season, all right.

IN THE UNDERCROFT of the church, Emilio was considerably better but still not ready for prime time. Not strong enough to go to work or even to the library or the coffee shop, he had become a virtual prisoner of the underground construction project. This was a mixed blessing. There was nothing to do but keep still. He could occupy himself on his phone as long as the battery held. He'd also taken some books out of the church library on one of his clandestine meanderings. These, he could read by the light of his camping lantern. Reading books in English and sounding out and looking up the words he didn't know was a way of improving himself and moving forward, even if he was trapped.

It was no way to live, but Emilio had no choice. It was this or the deportation police, and he was not about to abandon his dream.

UPSTAIRS in the chilly old church, Olympia made quick work of checking in with Gordy and Franklin, responding to phone messages, emails, and making the decision that the best use of her time would be on the road making pastoral visits in people's warm houses. This would all begin, however, with an unannounced visit to The Windjammer and a request for a little face-time with the manager.

The popular restaurant, only two miles from the church, was busy with a holiday lunch crowd. The setting was lovely, right on the fabled Loring harbor, with the surrounding sea water currently frozen into a slushy mess The few remaining pleasure boats hardly moved in the cold, bright sun, and the wind that blew over and around them was piercing. Olympia wasted no time in getting inside and asking to see the manager.

She was escorted to a table in the corner of the bar and asked if she would like anything to drink. "A cup of black coffee, please. It's punishingly cold out there. I need something hot."

"Right away, madam."

Within five minutes, the manager himself entered the room, carrying her coffee. He set it on the table and seated himself before introducing himself as Art Lavoie and asking how could he help her.

She wasted no time. "I'm Reverend Olympia Brown. I'm the woman who called you last week to say that Emilio Vieira was taken ill in my church last week, and he would be out of work for a while. That was Wednesday. By Friday, he'd left the hospital, and I have been trying to find him ever since. He was very ill, and I'm worried about him. I was wondering if you've heard from him. I want to help him."

The manager spoke carefully. "I'm glad to hear that. Emilio is a good man and a hard worker. He's as honest as the day is long. I've been worried about him too, but like you, I have no idea where he is. I'm sure he's undocumented. So many of these men and women who work in the hospitality industry are, and they keep a very low profile. I usually don't ask. I told him to come back to work when he can. He has called in to say he's better but not well enough to come in."

"If he calls in again, will you ask him to get in touch with me?" Olympia handed the man her card. "Please tell him I know some people who want to help him."

Lavoie looked at the card and pocketed it. "Thank you, Reverend. I wish more people wanted to help these folks. God knows they need and deserve it. I could tell you stories, but I have to get back to work."

"I'll bet you could, and I have to get on with my own day. Do please let me know if you hear from him."

"If he does call you, tell him his job is ready whenever he is."

Olympia stood and extended her hand. "Thank you so much, Mr. Lavoie. Emilio said you were a good man. He was right."

Lavoie smiled and extended his hand. "You take care, now."

Olympia climbed back into her van, continued on her

appointed rounds, and was pleased to find herself on the way home well before the day began to fade.

She blew in through the back door with tangled thoughts of the furnace-less church, her missing Brazilian, and Andrea and her children adding to her predictable anxieties about the annual children's Christmas pageant and the Christmas Eve candlelight service.

Frederick, ever sensitive to her temperament and moods, caught the troubled look and put on the kettle. "Tea first for you, my love. You can have your wine with supper, which, you will be pleased to know, Andrea and the girls are planning to surprise you with supper. Come on, then. Off with the coat and into the sitting room with you. Do not look at the stove or the countertop or try to smell anything good as you walk past."

Who could not be cheered by such a welcoming? She heard the girls whispering and giggling on the stairs. Andrea, a bit straggle-haired and wearing one of Olympia's aprons, was actually smiling as she stepped back to let Olympia pass. This was exactly what she needed and hoped no one would catch her blinking and wiping her eyes. On the other hand, so what if they did? She was home, wasn't she? And this was her new family.

THAT NIGHT, after the furnace was pronounced dead and the workmen cleared out, Emilio crept out of his cave. Constantly alert to any sound that might have been someone coming back into the building, he was able to plug in his phone and call his boss at the restaurant to say that he thought he could be in by Friday or Saturday at the latest. His boss told him to come back when he felt strong enough and gave him Olympia's number, saying only that she'd been in touch and wanted to help him, and would Emilio please call her when

he could? Emilio needed to think about that. By now, he
really did trust the reverend, and at the same time, he didn't
want to bother her with his troubles. Still, maybe...

The empty building was colder than the grave without
central heating, and he shivered. He wasted no time in going
upstairs to forage for some food and water and use the toilet
before returning to his hideout. There, below ground, the
temperature was marginally warmer. He was set for at least
another day but wondered how long this would continue.

26

Olympia woke up refreshed and hopeful. The night before, the kids had cooked up a supper of mac and cheese and hot dogs for the non-vegetarians and some boiled eggs for her. Dessert was chocolate ice cream with smashed-up Oreos on top for dessert. Comfort food never tasted so good, and she slept like a rock.

Now, well rested and in a much better frame of mind, she decided to take advantage of the early alone time with Andrea and see if she had any thoughts or had made any plans for after the holidays. With Christmas almost upon them and the week following it a virtual throwaway, it wouldn't hurt to see how she was progressing.

"I know one thing." Andrea put her coffee mug down on the table with a bit more force than might have been necessary. "Actually, I know two things. I talked to the police again yesterday about uh…final arrangements. Once they release the body, I will have him cremated and plan some sort of funeral later on, maybe even wait until spring."

"That's one," said Olympia. "What's two?"

"I already told you I'm not going back to the house we lived in for all the tea in China, so I need to find a place to live. I've decided to stay in Loring, at least for now. The kids have friends there, and they need to go back to school. Once I get them settled, I will go back into practice."

"That's a whole lot of two," said Olympia with a bit of a twinkle in her eye. "But it sounds altogether reasonable and practical. If it fits into your future plans, I'd love to have you start bringing the kids to church once in a while. No pressure, of course. We have a great program for children and families there, and you'll be able to make some connections for your-self as well."

"I have to find a place to live first. I'll need to rent in the beginning, but once I get rid of the mansion from hell, I can get something more suitable, something we can live in and not appear in." Her face flushed as she was finally beginning to voice the anger she'd worked so long and so hard to suppress.

Not the time to go there right now, thought Olympia, automatically slipping into pastor-mode. We both have too much to get through first. The time will come. I'll make sure of that. She looked up at the clock...the one that worked.

"Yikes, look at the time. I've got to get dressed and get out of here. I have to make a few stops on the way to work this morning, and who knows what I'll find when I get there? They're supposed to start installing the new furnace today. And I have been promised, God willing, it will be done by Christmas. It gives new meaning to the power of prayer, doesn't it?" She paused as a very bright light bulb went off inside her head, and

she held up an index finger.

"Christmas! Hah! How do you think the girls would like to dress up like angels and be in the annual children's pageant? There's always room for more angels, and all they have to do is stand there and look adorable. What do you think?"

Andrea broke into a smile that spread all over her face.

"Oh, my gosh. They would absolutely love that. I would too." She crossed her arms and hugged herself. "That would really give us something happy and fun to look forward to." She paused. "We could use it."

"Let me see what I can do. It shouldn't be a problem. I just need to find out when the rehearsal is and if there are enough costumes. If not, we can make them. They are little more than ghost sheets with sparkles and paper-plate haloes on headbands."

It was hard to say who was more excited about the idea.

"Okay then, I'm off," said Olympia. "You tell the kids. I'll make it happen."

On the way to work, Olympia caught herself singing, "It's beginning to look a lot like Christmas."

TRAPPED IN THE BASEMENT, Emilio had stuffed his ears with Kleenex against the metallic banging and clanging and ripping of metal, the sounds of the demolition and removal of the old furnace. He was beyond miserable and afraid he might go totally mad with it all…until it stopped, and all was silent. What now? He could hear nothing outside his crawl space. Nothing at all. Had they gone home? Were they coming back? Did he dare slip back the panel and look? He knew how to move it just enough to see into the original undercroft and not be seen by the casual observer—in the unlikely event that there was a casual observer in the vicinity.

He wiggled himself over to the secret panel and slipped it marginally to one side. So far, so good. No sounds of anyone moving or breathing. Nothing human. He edged it back a little further to where he could see something big and dark directly in front of the opening. He listened again, and when he heard nothing, he slowly reached out his hand to where he could touch a great pile of cardboard and packaging material. It was the new furnace, a couple of hundred pounds of it, leaning against the partition that was the outside wall of his living space. He tried pushing on it. Nothing. He removed the secret panel completely and leaned his shoulder against it. Still nothing. The thing was as heavy as a bucket of boulders, and Emilio Vieira, still with very little strength, was trapped. He fought hard to push down and control the rising panic. Think, Emilio. Think, and for God's sake, whatever you do, don't cough.

WRAPPED in multiple layers in her office, Olympia called Franklin and asked about the timeline for the installation of the new furnace. She was assured that he'd been promised it would be up and running by Saturday morning, just two days hence. Christmas Eve was on Sunday. The pageant was scheduled for four in the afternoon, followed by the annual candlelight and carol service at seven. With good planning, everyone would be all Christmassed-up and on their respective ways home by eight thirty at the latest. Things were looking up.

Gordy didn't work on Thursdays, and she was grateful to have the place to herself. Much as she loved having Andrea and the kids at the house, it did add a dimension of chaos, which made it hard to concentrate on things like a sermon. Thanks to the space heater, her church office was tolerable. And the rented generator did the honors of keeping the rest of the building well above freezing.

First on her list was to contact the most-blessed and ever-patient Corinne Garland, director of the children's program and this year's pageant. She knew that the woman would cheerfully welcome two new little angels, but courtesy and respect required that Olympia ask. She'd learned a long time ago that courtesy and respect opened doors, calmed troubled waters, and smoothed more than a few ruffled feathers. It was good ministry, and they didn't teach it in seminary.

Corrine's husband, Andrew Garland, was an honest-to-goodness professional opera singer, and each Christmas, he concluded the children's pageant by singing "Oh, Holy Night," and thereby reducing most of the congregation to tears. Their two daughters, Ava and Amara, would be the lead angels this year. They were the oldest children and the leaders of this year's heavenly host, responsible for directing and riding herd on the more rambunctious of the shepherds and angels, when and however possible, keeping them in line. A delicate balance. And yet, it was the predictable disasters that made each year's performance so memorable and so heartwarming. This was church at its very best: warm, human, flawed, and somehow, still perfect.

27

O lympia had just returned to her desk with her second cup of coffee when Franklin Bowen walked through the door. Olympia had long gotten over her first impression of the man. Conservative, yes, but open-minded with it, he passionately loved the building and the faith, in that order. The way to his New England Yankee heart was always through his pride of ownership of the edifice and its notable history. Olympia knew she would challenge him one day on some of that history, but today was not the day.

"I saw your car and decided to come in and see if you were warm enough. Now that I'm here, I think I'll go over and check on the parsonage as well. With it being empty and all, I need to keep an eye on it. You know, same thing as here, pipes and all. Critters too. Mice and such get in there in the cold weather. We had a squirrel family set up housekeeping in the attic a couple of years ago, and my God, didn't they make a mess." He shook his head and chuckled at the memory.

Olympia hadn't given much thought to the parsonage, a big old Victorian house that was a stone's throw from the church. She hadn't given it much of a thought until that very minute. They'd offered it to her when she took the job, but she had declined. Her own home was within easy commuting distance, so there was really no point. Besides, much as she loved her work, she had no desire to live within shouting distance of the church.

Another light bulb flashed in Olympia's brain. "So, Franklin, that big old house is just sitting there empty, right?"

He nodded.

"Has the church ever thought of renting it? It would be a great way to help with the cost of the upkeep of the place and not drain the church budget."

He frowned. "We've usually had the minister living in it. Can't say as we've ever thought about renting it. No point really. Too much hassle. Besides which, you'll only be here for another year, and we have to have it available for the settled minister."

It was not the time to tell him that more and more ministers preferred to have a modicum of privacy for themselves and their families rather than living under the watchful eyes of the entire congregation. She'd save that for later.

"You have something in mind?"

"I don't know. I can't help thinking it's really sad to have such a beautiful place just sitting there when so many people need housing."

Franklin shot her a wary look, and the temperature in the room dropped by at least twenty degrees.

"Reverend, the people who need housing can't usually afford the rent for a place like that. Most people in Loring own their homes. Actually, we don't encourage rentals. This is a place for people who want to put down roots and stay, not for transients."

"I see," said Olympia.

"I knew you would."

Boy, do I, thought Olympia.

"All in a day's work. Now, I'm going to run next door and give the place a once-over. If everything's okay, I'll go straight home. We're having our annual neighborhood Christmas party tonight, and my husband is bouncing off the walls."

"I totally understand," said the good reverend. And by God, she did.

After he left, Olympia didn't know whether to laugh or cry, or stamp her foot and throw something. Much as she liked and respected Franklin, there were times she simply wanted to shake him. Now was one of them. How, she asked herself, could he, a man who had lived a life of marginalization because of his own lifestyle and gender preference, be so damnably exclusive when it came to people who still struggled? I've got some work to do, she told herself, but I'm not sure whether I'll get very far. On the other hand, isn't the job of any good minister to comfort the afflicted and afflict the comfortable? It was a rhetorical question.

She double-checked the calendar. Thursday: three more days to Christmas Eve. Her homily wasn't finished, the number of holiday houseguests was increasing by the day, and she'd just hatched a plan for where Andrea and the girls might set up housekeeping after the holidays. Weren't churches supposed to serve as sanctuaries for people in need and under threat? Andrea could afford to pay a reasonable rent, and it wouldn't be permanent. Didn't she say just that morning that she wanted a place of her own, a more modest place, and that she wanted to stay in Loring? Olympia rubbed her chin and smiled. Maybe this wouldn't be such a long shot after all.

She was trying to decide whether to go home and start drafting a strategy or stay put where, even if it was a bit chilly around the edges, she would have privacy, and then her cell phone rang.

"Hello, this is Reverend Olympia."

"Reverend?" an unfamiliar voice croaked. "I need help."

"Oh, my God, Emilio, is that you? Where are you? Are you all right? I'm so worried. Where are you?"

A long, ragged breath. "I am here in the church…down in the old cellar. Near furnace. I'm stuck behind something big, and I can't get out. I'm afraid."

"Oh, Jesus! Don't hang up. I'll be right down."

Olympia shoved the phone in her pocket, raced down the stairs to the old part of the cellar, and pushed open the door.

"Emilio, where are you?"

"In here, behind the boxes. I can't move them. I can't get out." The fear in his voice was heartbreaking.

She leaned forward and pushed with all her strength on the carton, but it was immoveable.

"Hold on. I'll think of something. I'm here, and I'm going to get you out of there. You have air to breathe. You'll be all right."

"Don' call police."

"Emilio, I told you I wouldn't. I just need to get you out, and I don't know how." She paused, "Wait a minute. Maybe I do. It'll take a few minutes, but I'm going to call my husband. He works in a bookstore here in Loring. Don't be afraid. Please trust me, Emilio. I want to help you. I want to help you bring your family here."

"Okay. I wait… *obrigado*, thank you." Even through the wall, his voice sounded calmer and maybe even a little bit stronger. Or was that just wishful thinking?

Within minutes, she'd contacted her two men. Frederick was immediately on his way and would be there shortly. Jim would take longer, but she needed him there as well. Now, her only concern was that Franklin, Gordy, or some other well-meaning member of the church community would decide that this was the time to drop in and wish her a Merry Christmas. Please, God!

It was only then that she asked the obvious question: how in the world did Emilio get into the crawl space? That was one more holy mystery she would have to explore. Right now, her job was to get the man out of there and see to his health and safety. This, she could do. And as crazy as this all was, things were looking up. Christmas always was a time for miracles. Let's see if this one is any exception, she asked herself. Then she went back to talking to Emilio through the wall and the pile of boxes and cartons.

"Reverend? You talking to someone down there?" It was Franklin.

"Shit!" said the reverend under her breath as the man came through the old wood-plank door.

"You're back. I thought you were going home."

"I came back for my hat, and I heard your voice. What in the world are you doing down here? I heard voices. Everything's okay next door in the parsonage, and I think we ought to think about maybe looking it over after the holidays. You know, maybe spruce it up a little for the new minister. I wouldn't mind your opinion."

Jesus H. Christ, will you get the hell out of here?

"Let's talk about that upstairs." She tried to lead him out, but he wouldn't budge.

"First, tell me what in the world you are doing down here. You could have tripped over something or fallen and hurt yourself, and you'd be here overnight before anyone found you. Now that's just not sensible, Reverend. What were you thinking, and who were you talking to?"

"I, uh." Olympia plastered her most wide-eyed and innocent minister face on the front of her head. "Myself. I was talking to myself. I wanted to see it firsthand. I would have come down earlier, but with all that noise and the workmen and everything, I would have been in the way. I've never been in this part of the cellar. It's, uh…really old."

"Like I told you, all the way back to 1789. Boy, if these old stones could talk."

I'm really glad they can't right now, thought Olympia, *and don't start now,* she mentally warned them.

"Well, now that I've seen it, let's get out of here. You've

got a house party to prepare for, and …oh, yes, my husband and my clergy-buddy, Father Jim, are going to meet me here in a little bit. We thought we'd go check out The Wind-jammer for dinner before the holiday madness completely takes over."

They both walked out of the cellar, and Franklin pulled the door shut with a *bang* behind them.

"I'm going to lock the outside door when I leave. I don't like the idea of you being alone in an empty building."

Oh, but it's not empty, thought Olympia with a secret smile.

"Good idea, Franklin. I'll call Frederick and tell him to ring the bell when he gets here."

"Well, I may or may not see you before Sunday afternoon, but if you need anything, you know where to find me."

"I do indeed. You take care now, and if you know what's good for you, you'd better get home if you are going to be ready for that party of yours. And Franklin… thanks for everything you do."

Frederick's startlingly yellow 1950 Ford pickup was turning into the parking lot when Franklin drove off and down the street. He had been at the bookstore, which was less than a half hour away from the church. She gave him a quick hug and asked him to wait upstairs for Jim, who she thought would be along within the hour. She went back downstairs to wait with Emilio.

When Jim arrived, it took the combined efforts of the three of them to wrestle the boxes containing the new furnace and all of its component parts far enough to one side to set Emilio free. He emerged, his face dirty and tear streaked, from underneath the derelict stairwell to the cheers and applause of his three sweaty saviors. Emilio wiped away another renegade tear and allowed himself to be pulled upright.

"Hold on," said Olympia. "We're not done yet."

The three men stopped and waited for instructions.

"With the exception of Emilio, who needs all of his strength standing on his feet, we have to put everything back exactly the way we found it. Nothing out of place. Nothing to make anyone ask even one teensy little question. Then I'll do the introductions."

28

P erhaps it was the encouragement and assurance of Father Jim, wearing his clerical collar, or the man with the English accent who looked so kindly at him. Perhaps it was the utter desperation of his situation or the fact that Reverend Olympia had once again come to his aid that he finally decided to trust her. Whatever it was, and likely it was all three, Emilio cautiously agreed to go and stay with Olympia and Frederick in Brookfields until he was well enough to return to work.

First came a detour to The Windjammer to check in with the manager in person and decide how and when Emilio should return to work. With that accomplished, they set out, four people in three cars, all heading south. Olympia didn't like the obvious metaphor but said nothing.

Emilio sat in Olympia's van with his arms around his backpack and stared at the road ahead. He was a proud man. Accepting help was not easy for him. Accepting help from a woman was even harder. Not having any choices was the hardest of all. He knew she was a good woman. She'd proved it to him, over and over again. And her friend, the priest, was a good man. Her husband, the one with the accent, seemed friendly enough, but Emilio really didn't know any of them. He watched the streetlights flash by, and then, trying to keep himself awake, he started counting them.

Meanwhile, Olympia was doing her best to prepare him for what awaited him when they got home. Where to start? Two cats and the widow of a murder victim and her twin daughters? A two-hundred-plus-year-old dwelling, a well-meaning and protective house ghost? Jim drove the third car and would join them for dinner that evening and again on Christmas Day—her best friend in the world: a gay, partnered Anglican priest. Where to begin on that lot, she asked herself, and decided to start with the most pressing and most potentially volatile: Andrea and the twins.

As she drove, she turned the car radio on to classical music to provide some background pleasantry to fill in the empty spaces when neither of them wanted to talk. Over the half-hour drive, Olympia told Emilio about the house and its collection of occupants, a little about her ministry, and the reason why she offered him hospitality and safety in her home.

Talking was still an effort for Emilio, but in bits and pieces, he told her more about his family and his dreams and how he came to be living in the church cellar. She told him that once she'd learned of his situation in the hospital, she'd asked her friend Jim to get some information on immigration law and that they would do all in their power to help him.

She did not tell him that she'd learned that he might be a person of interest in the murder and that the police were looking for him. What good would it do? It would only serve to shred the thin fabric of trust she was so carefully weaving. No, there was no need to say anything about that yet.

She did explain that Andrea, the mother of the twins, had lived in Loring, and she'd left home with her two children the day before her husband was murdered.

Olympia slowed and turned into the drive. "Home sweet

home," she said more to herself than her drowsy passenger. She knew full well that getting him out of the church cellar and into the light was the end of one story, but it was also the beginning of another. There were too many unanswered questions, too many knots to untangle, and she had no idea where the lead string was hiding nor where it would take her once she found it.

Meanwhile, she had an undocumented, physically and mentally exhausted Brazilian immigrant sitting next to her holding on to most, if not all, of his American earthly possessions, a man she would shortly introduce to a family still in shock from their own traumas. After the introductions, she'd break the news to them that he, too, was moving in. Merry Christmas everybody!

What the hell am I thinking? Never mind, woman. It's too late to think. Just get on with it.

Olympia led the weary group through the back door into the warm, chaotic kitchen. The twins were busy making paper snowflakes, and the place looked like a blizzard had struck. Andrea sat with them, looking dazed and anxious. Olympia put on her cheery, I'm-going-to-convince-you-of-something-you-might-not-be-too-sure-of face. The cats, sensing the tension, removed themselves to the peace and quiet of the sitting room.

"Andrea, this is Emilio. He comes to the church sometimes." She paused. "Long story. He needs a place to stay for a little while. I'm going to put him up in my office. Emilio, this is Andrea and her two daughters." She pointed first to one and then the other. "That's MaryBeth, and that's Julianne."

"We're twins," said MaryBeth.

"And I'm the oldest," rejoined Julianne.

"They've been making snowflakes and covering the floor with scraps, I'm afraid," said their weary mother.

Olympia waved her arms in a grand, encompassing

gesture. "These aren't scraps. I thought we were having our own private snowstorm in here. Not a problem. That's why God made brooms."

Emilio watched all of this, and aside than nodding his head in greeting and acknowledgement, he said nothing.

A second look at Andrea told Olympia that something was wrong. Very wrong.

"Andrea, if you don't mind, can you come help me get some things down from upstairs?" She turned to Frederick and Jim. "And you two, can you show Emilio where he'll be sleeping. While you're in there, pull out the sofa bed and fluff up the blankets and pillows. I keep it made up, but we'll likely need an extra blanket and towels and stuff. That's what I need Andrea for."

Without waiting for any kind of a response, Olympia hurried Andrea out of the room on the pretext of getting things for Emilio. Once upstairs and out of earshot she didn't wait, but immediately asked to know what was so clearly troubling her guest.

Andrea covered her face with her two hands and fought for control. When she'd achieved it, she spoke. "About an hour before you got home, I got a call from a woman at Boston Police Headquarters. They want to question me as part of the investigation into my husband's murder. First of all, how did Boston get into it? He was killed in Loring." She frowned and counted on her fingers.

"Second of all, what's this all about, anyway? They were treating me as though I was a suspect in this whole thing. How's that for the American justice system? I only wanted to get away from James—from everything in that awful house." She added another finger.

"And third of all, yes, I hated him, but dammit, I didn't kill him. So what do they want with me?" Her fear and frustration and anger were inextricably tangled, and for the first time since Olympia met the woman, she wanted to jump up and down and cheer. Finally, she thought, the woman is showing some emotion, some spunk. That's what I've been looking for. Now she can start to move forward. All of this, Olympia kept to herself.

"Andrea, did they say when they wanted to meet with you?"

"That's just it," she wailed. "They didn't really give me an option. They said they asked the Loring detectives how to get in touch with me and then asked to come over here tonight. They said it wouldn't take long."

"What!"

Andrea nodded. "I figured if I had to talk to them, I might as well just get it over with. Anyway, it's too late now."

"Did they say when they were coming?" Olympia thought of Emilio and his fear of the police and anything connected to law enforcement.

"I'm sorry. I should have asked, but I didn't know you were bringing people back for dinner."

Olympia shook her head and held up her hand. She didn't have much time. "You didn't do anything wrong. And you're right. Get it over with, and put it to rest. It's Emilio I'm worried about. He's the man I told you about, the man who collapsed in the church last week and who we took to the hospital. I'm trying to help him. I'll tell you everything later, but right now, I have to get Emilio out of here, and I have to keep him out until after the police have come and gone. If he sees a uniform in this house, he'll go ballistic. He'll think I lied to him and set a trap."

Olympia handed a stack of towels to Andrea. "Here, you take these, and grab a blanket and a face cloth and bring them downstairs. I have to get Emilio out of here right this minute."

"But, Olympia, I was hoping you'd be there when they questioned me. I mean, you don't know me well, but you do know me, and you're a minister. They can't think I had anything to do with it. Can they?"

Olympia wanted to scream. Crisis in stereo, in surround sound. Merry Freaking Christmas.

She patted the woman's arm. "Okay, hang in there. I'll stay and have Jim and Frederick take Emilio out. But I have to do it right this minute."

Olympia turned and raced down the stairs. No time for the niceties, and she hated lying, but there were times when she had no other option. She could only hope that Jim or Frederick didn't start questioning her abrupt change in behavior.

She quick-stepped into the kitchen. "Jim, Frederick. I need some supper shopping, and I need it now. I meant to stop on the way home from work, but in all the excitement, I forgot."

Both men picked up on her look and her tone of voice. Something was very wrong or about to be.

"And, why don't you take Emilio along with you. He can help, I'm sure. We need lots of things…and… I, uh…" She flicked her eyes in the direction of the stairs to the second floor. "I have to stay here with Andrea. She needs some private time…minister time with me…right now. Say, why don't you all go over to that really nice market off Exit 6. I know it's a little bit further away, but it's got such nice stuff. Call me when you get there, and I'll give you the list. I didn't write it down. I'm sure Emilio would enjoy picking some things out as well—maybe some Brazilian things."

She was trying her best to look cheery and nonchalant, but Jim and Frederick knew her well enough to see through the pretense. They also picked up on the implication that this was not a time for questions. There was a reason she wanted them all out of there right that very minute. Like a well-oiled machine, Jim and Frederick handed Emilio back his jacket and hat, and the two all but quick-marched him out the door.

All the while, the two of them were loudly and mannishly complaining about having to do all the work. Not only did they have to cook, but she made them do the shopping as well. If Emilio suspected anything, he was too tired and dazed to protest.

EMILIO LIKED food and he enjoyed cooking. Maybe, when he didn't feel so weak and tired, he would cook a Brazilian meal for everyone. In that moment, he realized he was getting better. Yes, he was tired, but for the first time in over a week, he was actually thinking about something that was not centered on merely staying alive and keeping under the radar. He allowed himself to be folded into the back seat of Jim's Corolla, and despite his best efforts, fell instantly and deeply asleep.

29

The good news was Frederick, Jim, and Emilio were well out of sight when the black-and-white police car arrived. Olympia's house was a back-door house. Friends and family came in through the kitchen door. Salesmen, solicitors, the Mormons and Jehovah's Witnesses, and now two Boston Police detective investigators respectfully used the front.

Olympia answered the door, introduced herself, and directed Detectives Esther Lim and Brooks Lawrence into the sitting room. Fortunately, they were not in uniform, and their presence would not alarm the children. They accepted the offer of coffee. This was a good sign, thought Olympia, who went on to say that while they were having their conversation, she would be in the next room, keeping the children occupied. Brooks and Esther thanked her and asked if she would please go and get the widow.

"She has a name. It's Doctor Andrea Riggs. I'll go and get her."

IN MINUTES, Andrea entered the room and closed the door

firmly behind her before taking a seat. The two detectives introduced themselves, offered their condolences, and thanked her for being so cooperative at such a difficult and trying time.

Much as she didn't want to, she withheld the snarky response to their formulaic and gratuitous opening words. She was simply too tired to play word games, mind games, or anything else, for that matter.

Esther wasted no time in getting to the point. "Dr. Riggs, as you know, we are investigating the murder of your husband. We know he was a highly successful cardiologist, but other than that, we've not had much luck in learning anything about his personal life."

"So that's where I come in, right? His personal life. That's a joke." She held up a defensive hand and started over. "Sorry, I didn't mean to snap. I'm not myself. And honestly, I'm not sure how much I can tell you. He lived his own life. He decided I would give up my practice, stay home, and look after the kids and the house. He ate breakfast and some dinners at home, but mostly, he came in after the girls were in bed. I don't think he liked being a husband and a father. I think we disturbed his life more than we added to it."

"Was he like that when you married him?"

Andrea thought for a moment. "He was a quiet man, and I'm pretty much of an introvert, so quiet was okay with me. But over the years, he started to change."

"When did he start abusing you?"

Andrea bit her lip and didn't respond. She wasn't ready for such a direct attack. She felt her eyes prickle, but she blinked away the tears that were trying to escape.

"Almost from the beginning," she whispered.

"Why did you stay? You had children with him? It couldn't have been all bad." Esther's tone was gentler now.

Andrea shook her head. "I didn't have children by him. I conceived the twins through in-vitro fertilization. We used a sperm donor, but he never wanted anyone to know. I thought having children would make up for what I wasn't giving him. It turned out to be exactly the opposite. That was when the abuse started getting really bad. And to answer your next question, I was terrified of him. He said if I ever tried to leave, he'd kill me, and he'd do it in front of the girls. I absolutely hated the man for what he was doing to us, but I didn't dare challenge him. I didn't care about myself anymore, but I did care about the girls. I couldn't do it to them."

"What finally did it?"

Andrea pulled the scarf off her head and pointed to the scabbed-over bald patch. Both detectives gasped.

"That's what did it. He knocked me down on the kitchen floor, put his foot on my neck and yanked. I thought my whole head was going to come off. It certainly felt that way. And then he raped me."

It took a few minutes for either detective to speak.

"Didn't the kids hear anything?"

She gave a derisive snort. "Are you kidding? He'd wait until they were asleep, shut their door and the door to the kitchen, then tell me if I made so much as a sound, he'd do it again." She was crying openly now. "He was a monster, and I'm glad he's dead, but I didn't do it."

"No, I don't think you did, but did you arrange for it to happen?"

"What!"

"You do understand that more than one abused spouse has arranged for such a thing to happen. I'm not saying you did, but we do have to ask. We have to explore every possibility, check out every suspicion, question everyone involved. It's what we get paid for."

Andrea looked back and forth between the two of them in disbelief.

"Are you telling me I'm a suspect?"

"No, Dr. Riggs, we are not. We do have to ask unpleasant

questions, and I'm afraid we have a few more."

Andrea held up her hand and shook her head. "Not tonight, you don't. I'm done. I don't want to answer any more questions, and I want a lawyer present when or if I do. And before you tell me, I'll tell you. I'm not going anywhere. I'm not running away from this. There's nothing for me to run away from. I ran away. Once was enough."

She stood up and waited for them to do the same.

They did.

"Understood. Thank you for meeting with us, Doctor. Oh, yes, and as a formal courtesy, you should know we've obtained a search warrant for the domestic residence."

Andrea was caught totally off guard.

"That is a total outrage and invasion of privacy," she snapped. "I don't want strange people going through my things." She was shouting now, and Olympia stuck her head through the door.

"Are you all right, Andrea?"

"I most certainly am not, but it seems there's nothing either of us can do about it right now. Thank you anyway."

Olympia gave her a cautious thumbs-up and withdrew.

Andrea turned back to the two detectives. "And what, may I ask, are you looking for?"

"Drugs, Dr. Riggs."

"Well, of course, you're going to find drugs. He's…he was a doctor. He had samples of all kinds of drugs. All doctors get them."

"No, ma'am, I mean drugs…street-trade. We have reason to believe that your husband may have been involved in the drug trade."

Stunned, Andrea dropped back into her chair. "Oh, my God. Of course. The mood swings, the insane hours, the irregular sleep patterns, strange phone calls. Good God, how on earth could I have missed it?"

"Sometimes, the wife is the last to know, Dr. Riggs."

In the supermarket, Emilio followed Jim and Frederick up and down the colorful and well-stocked aisles. The short nap had temporarily revived him, and leaning on the cart as they meandered made walking less difficult. He was always overwhelmed by the sight of such plenty—overwhelmed and amazed. He would bring his family here, to this everyday abundance, whatever it took.

Frederick and Jim knew their task was to keep Emilio safe and unaware of whatever was unfolding back at the house. They knew that Olympia would call them when it was safe to return, and they wondered how long they would have to drag this poor, tired man around the store, or, if it went on much longer, where they would take him next. But despite everything that was going on beneath the surface, the men enjoyed themselves. Jim and Frederick consulted Emilio as to what they should add to the basket and included him in their exaggerated grumbling about Olympia and how she was always pushing them around. Emilio listened, and from time to time, he even smiled.

Then, as the three were beginning to run out of idle chatter, Frederick's cell phone rang. It was Olympia telling them the coast was clear, and they could come home.

"And pick up a couple of pizzas, will you? A plain cheese for the kids, an all veggie for me, and whatever else you fancy. I can make up a salad with what I've got here. We have milk, beer, and wine, and I've got ice cream in the freezer."

She also explained why she rushed them out of the house on such short notice and thanked them for not asking why.

This time, Emilio didn't fall asleep in the car. For the first time in well over a week, he was starving. He'd managed a quick wash-up in one of the church bathrooms before they set out, but now, as hungry as he was, he was even more desperate for a long, hot, full-body, soapy shower.

30

Detectives Lawrence and Lim were on the South East Expressway, heading north and comparing notes. Detective Lim cheerfully exceeded the speed limit as they drove back to BPD headquarters.

"So what do you think?" she asked.

"Hard to say. I do believe she was clueless about his drug involvement. Cabot seems to have been a vicious, calculating son of a bitch, who knew how to cover his tracks, both at home and at work."

"Until the day he didn't."

"Or he got so drugged up himself, he screwed up and got caught."

"So what do you think about her?" Lim glanced up at the rearview mirror.

"She's been through shit. Deep shit. You have to wonder how she managed. Sometimes, people snap."

"Do you think she did it? Hey, do you have to drive this fast?"

She ignored the warning. "Nobody else gets to do this and get away with it. Consider it a perk."

"Slow down, and answer my question. Do you think she's involved?"

"I don't, but I'm not ready to take her off the list either. It's when she demanded that a lawyer be present is when the warning signals went up. She's holding on to something."

"Agreed."

"What's next?"

Lim frowned. "I think we need to have a look around the hospital. We really are working on part one of a two-part case, you know. One is the murder, and two, the bigger issue, not that murder isn't big enough, is the whole drug thing. That's in a whole different category. This is not one man who's become addicted and was dealing on the side for a little pocket change. We're looking at organized crime. And it's not only Boston. Cabot is collateral damage. He got in some-body's way. From what I hear, this may reach all the way across the country—and beyond."

"Jesus. How long has this particular drug investigation been going on?"

"Well over a year now, but it's all undercover. If they go public with it before they are ready to crack it open, the big boys will slither underground like the snakes they are."

"The things you don't learn at staff briefings." He shook his head.

"Not our department. We're working on the murder with the Loring guys, but unlike them, we are looking at it in rela-tion to the drug connection. So what else do we need?"

"Ballistics report. Assorted forensics and then the house search. We'll likely have a few more questions for the Widow Riggs after that, wouldn't you say?"

"I'd say."

AN AWKWARD GROUP of people sat around Olympia's kitchen

table that night after the detectives left. Two of them were persons of interest in an open murder case, one, an undocumented immigrant, the other, an emotionally exhausted recent widow of a murdered doctor. Add to that the widow's twin daughters and a lady minister who couldn't stop herself from dragging home and caring for people in need. Beside her sat her dearest and most trusted friend, an Anglican priest, a man who had a confidential legal information line through a childhood friend, now a Dorchester cop. Cautiously padding around underneath all of this were two seriously indulged cats. Seven humans and three times that number of stories and secrets and burdens they carried in their hearts.

BOING-BOING!

And a watchful clock doing her best to issue a warning to the people in the next room.

OLYMPIA WAS hard-pressed to keep the conversation moving. Emilio, despite that fact that his color was better and his voice stronger, was clearly exhausted. Andrea had just been through the wringer, courtesy of two Boston Police detectives. The two children, as kids always are, were well aware of the tension in the room but were completely ignorant of its multiple layers. So they did what all kids do when they're unsure of themselves. They alternated between saying nothing and poking each other under the table and whispering secret messages into their mother's ear. Then, without warning, they would pivot away into silliness and eventually, into knock-knock jokes. It was the kids and knock-knock jokes that eventually broke the tension and saved the evening.

Emilio didn't know what a knock-knock joke was. They didn't have such a thing in Brazil, he told them. Then he asked if they could tell him what they were. Needless to say, two bright-eyed little girls fell into fits of laughter over

Emilio's Brazilian lack of understanding. This, plus the ridiculous content of the jokes themselves were precisely what everyone needed. It was time out of time and something everyone could join in on.

Between mispronouncing half the words, trying to explain the subtleties of something that has no subtlety whatsoever, and making up new jokes that were equally sophomoric, the cautious barriers of unfamiliarity slowly melted away. By the time Emilio and the girls went off to their beds, the smiles and the good-night hugs that went around the table were genuine and heartfelt.

Jim winked at Olympia across the table and then announced that, much as he'd like to stay and do the dishes for everyone, it was high time he got on the road and headed for home.

"Otherwise, I'll have some explaining to do." He said this with a fond smile and an exaggerated eye-roll. "For some reason, it's okay for Andrew to keep late hours, maybe because he's a musician. But I'm a priest, and my day starts in the morning, so I can't. He likes to have me there when he gets home. It's been a long time since anyone cared."

Now it was Olympia's turn to smile and wink.

31

F or Olympia, the days running up to Christmas Eve and Christmas Day were a mostly happy mix of intense professional minister work at the church and pleasantly chaotic pre-Christmas frivolity at home.

At church, miracle of miracles, the new furnace was installed and working as it was supposed to. The choir and the pageant kids were jostling for time and space to practice. Gordon Bennett fussed about all of the disorder, but that's what he did. Olympia had long since learned to work around it.

Predictably, requests for pastoral care and counseling increased as the holiday pressures mounted on young and old, single and partnered. So sad, she thought, as she listed the calls she needed to make, that the season that was supposed to be all about peace on earth, good will toward all, was often anything but. She knew that Christmas could be one of the loneliest times of the year and that comfort and joy were empty words for far too many. And then, Olympia knew she had the title for her Christmas homily: "Simple Gifts." Be grateful for the little things, and try to keep the big ones in perspective.

On the home front, it was all good, or at least it looked, sounded, and smelled that way. Olympia knew there were moments when Andrea needed to go off by herself and when Emilio's eyes filled with tears, times when the girls forgot that their father was dead and had to be reminded. But all together, for this Christmas, they were a newly constructed temporary family, and as such, they all looked out for each other.

Andrea and the girls offered to do most of the holiday baking. Emilio, who was cautiously feeling more and more a part of everything, offered to make some Brazilian holiday dishes. And despite the limited amount of time left to them, there were piles of secret things, papers and ribbons everywhere. The cats were in kitty heaven with so many things to chase, pounce on, and hide under.

There was lots of giggling, and firm directives like, "don't look behind that door," or "stay out of that closet," were constant. Frederick had banned everyone from his workshop in the barn, but they all wondered at the curious thumps and bangs and twangs heard from behind that door.

When asked, he simply smiled. "Christmas secrets."

And so it was, with all of its tinseled anticipation, the days were accomplished, and Christmas Eve arrived and gently gathered them all into its mystery.

The much-heralded children's pageant, scheduled to begin at four, was of course, running late. That too was part of the tradition. But by a quarter after the appointed hour, the angel chorus, singing "Hark the Herald Angels Sing," wobbled down the center aisle.

Leading the adorable procession were Ava and Amara Garland, each one holding on to the hand of a redheaded six-year-old twin resplendent in a brand-new angel suit. Olympia, sentimental tears in free fall, sat with Emilio in one of the side pews. The center pews were reserved for proud parents and grandparents, all with cameras. This was not her show. This was all about the kids. She would have her turn later, but now, let the magic unfold.

The angels took their places across the back of a raised platform at the front: lead angels in the middle, a twin on either side, and the rest of the kids, arm's length apart, fanning out from there. After two verses of "While Shepherds Watched their Flocks," a ragged cluster of shepherds in bathrobes, both boy and girl shepherds, several carrying fuzzy, stuffed sheep-dolls and the odd teddy bear, entered from either side and sat down in front of the angels. This was carefully arranged to keep them well out of angelic kicking or poking distance. For insurance purposes, the shepherds' crooks had been quietly eliminated some years earlier. More carols, followed by the five wise people. Other than the roles of Mary and Joseph, which were chosen by lottery, the kids could be whatever they wanted, and consequently, the number of kings, the part with the best costumes, was often more of a flexible committee than a predictable threesome. This year, there were five of them, three boys and two girls, and not a single one of them tripped. "We three kings of Orient are…." They were led in by yet another angel waving a sequined star high up in front of her on a fishing rod.

"Oh, Little Town of Bethlehem" was the entrance cue for Mary and Joseph, and this year, they carried a real baby. Corrine Garland, the pageant director, artfully disguised as a much taller shepherd, stayed close by, hovered really, as they entered and took their places center stage.

"Away in a Manger" followed by "Silent Night" were the lead-up carols to the high point of the event. Ava and Amara's dad, Andrew Garland, also dressed as a shepherd, waited in the shadows until the lights were dimmed and only the flickering candles could be seen. Then he stepped forward and sang "Oh Holy Night." He sang it to the shepherds and to the angels and the holy family with their new baby. He sang to a recent widow and an undocumented Brazilian and a skeptical Englishman and a tearful minister. In that candlelit moment, a curious little patchwork of a put-together family understood that something greater than themselves was at work here, and for each one of them, it was enough.

AFTER THE PAGEANT, Andrea decided to take the girls back to the house. They were simply too excited and wound up to sit through another service.

"They'll still be up when we get home, won't they?" asked Frederick. He was loving every minute of this.

"I'm not sure. They're pretty excited, but they're also exhausted," said a weary-but-smiling Andrea. "They may have just lost their father, but this is the first real Christmas they've ever had. It's sad when you think about it." She corrected herself. "Sad, yes, but that was then, and this is now, and it's beyond wonderful. Thank you, my reverend friend." She threw her arms around Olympia, gave her a giant full-body hug, and gently herded the girls out into the cold and starlit night.

OLYMPIA STOOD for a moment to wave her off and saw a white SUV coast to a stop across the street directly in front of the main door. It remained there until Andrea pulled out onto the road, and when she passed, it pulled out and drove off in the same direction.

She gave it a brief second thought but quickly dismissed it as undoubtedly someone looking for something and not finding it. She shivered in the night cold, closed the front door, and walked back through the sanctuary to the church kitchen. She planned to have a bite to eat with Frederick and Emilio in the kitchen and then go back into her office to prepare for the candlelight carol service and to celebrate the simple gifts of being.

32

Olympia, Frederick, and Emilio, were back in Brookfields shortly after nine and walked in to a quiet and orderly house. The kids were already tucked into bed, totally exhausted from everything Christmas. The milk and cookies for Santa were in place, and their brightly colored stockings, hung and stuffed by Santa-Mom, were bulging with little surprises. Andrea took it upon herself to explain to Emilio about the milk and cookies and the stockings. In return, he told them about Papai Noel, who brings gifts to Brazilian children, and the folktale, where the shepherdesses, not the shepherds, protect the Christ-child from evil-minded gypsies who want to steal him.

The day was winding down, and so were the grownups. It was time for bed. Tomorrow would be a full and exciting day, and a good night's sleep would make it even better.

After Emilio and Andrea went off to their separate rooms, Frederick put his arm around his wife and suggested they have a quiet glass of wine together by the fire.

"It's not that I don't enjoy having a house full," he said with a fond smile, "but I'm missing quiet time with you."

"I know what you mean. This is great, but I miss you too."

Later, after the wine and the quiet conversation, Frederick took himself to bed, and Olympia picked up the diary. She needed a little quiet time with Leanna.

LATE DECEMBER, 1865

Cold and lovely today. I must confess, I am so very grateful to be back in my home in Brookfields. Having made the decision to return, I was pleased that Susan, Nathan, and Lottie were most eager to accompany me. They had the choice to remain in Cambridge but declined. Whatever we are and whatever the future may bring, for this precious time, we are a family. I had neither a sister nor a brother growing up, and was, I am told, a most startling surprise in my parents' middle years. As such, I grew up without brothers and sisters and spent my time in the company of people much older than myself. Now I find I am most, most grateful for this unexpected gift. It will indeed be a happy Christmas and a beautifully snowy one as well. Not too much, but just enough to give everything a fresh clean appearance. Little Annabelle called it angel dust. Such a darling little girl.

Richard is overjoyed that we are here. I have yet to explain to Susan and Lottie the full extent of our curious relationship. In due time. I must say that Richard was even more excited than the children. Within an hour of our arrival, he was at the kitchen door with a tree for us to decorate. And I add, he had the kindness and grace to bring a bucket of rocks to keep it well watered and solidly upright. Were he not so otherwise inclined, he would make a wonderful husband.

His secret is safe with me.

More anon….LFW

33

O lympia had more reasons than she could count for not feeling like leaving the house on Christmas morning. Once every seven years or so, Christmas Day fell on a Sunday. As such, it is probably the least well-attended service of the year. On those Sundays, Olympia usually did her version of a Ceremony of Carols. She planned an hour or so of seasonal music woven around and through a series of poems, prayers, and readings that reflected the holiday and the larger solstice message of bringing back and welcoming in the light of hope and faith.

As it was, she had more than enough time at home with everyone to enjoy the magic of the day through the eyes of the twins before she left. The service was at 10:30. It was short and sweet, and she would still be back in time for Christmas dinner.

In the days leading up to Christmas, Andrea had made it clear that while there would be presents for the children under the tree, and their stockings could indeed be hung by the chimney with care, she did not want this to be a gifts-out-of-sight and cash-out-of-pocket extravaganza. Frederick, Olympia, and even Emilio reluctantly agreed. Sort of. They also agreed to do the grown-up gifts and surprises after dinner in the afternoon so the kids could have the Christmas morning magic all to themselves.

Needless to say, the twins were out of bed by six and clamoring to go downstairs. Andrea, knowing that Olympia and the others had had a late night, held them back until she smelled coffee and knew someone else was up. Then, holding on to each of their hands, she led them down the stairs to the applause and cheers of her three housemates. Frederick and Olympia stood in the middle of the kitchen with Emilio positioned slightly behind them.

Frederick clapped his hands three times and bellowed, "My Lords and ladies, I've set out some coffee and bagels and cream cheese in the sitting room. The camera is poised and ready. The tree is lighted. The cats are trying to de-decorate the tree as we speak, and I hereby declare that it's time for the merriment to begin."

The kids, incandescent with excitement, stayed close to their mother, waiting to be told what to do.

"Do you want to start with your stockings or with what's been left under the tree?"

"The tree, the tree."

"Go ahead then. Each of you can go over and find a package with your name on it and come back here and unwrap it."

Olympia, her own impatience getting the better of her, wanted to scream, "Will you, for God's sake, turn them loose?" But she didn't. They weren't her children, and she knew Andrea had her reasons. The children were every bit as excited as Olympia's own two children had once been. Her eyes prickled at the sweet and distant memory, and then just as quickly, she flashed back to the kids in front of her.

After lunch and before the genuine English plum pudding, the pulling and snapping of traditional Christmas crackers, and other assorted holiday rituals, they would do their family gifts. It was Andrea's idea.

"That way," she said, "we can make it last longer, and everything won't get lumped together. Each one will be special."

She's not just a pretty face, thought Olympia. It was an excellent idea.

The kids got through their gifts, four each, and then they dove into their stockings. Olympia never did think it was fair to put socks and mittens and a brand-new toothbrush in a Christmas stocking. She remembered hiding her own disappointment at finding an orange and some nuts in her stocking one year. Funny, it never happened again. She looked at her watch. Yikes! It was time to go to work.

In her absence, Frederick, Emilio, and Andrea would clean up the first round of holiday clutter and set the scene for the next. With Jim and Andrew arriving after one that afternoon, there would be eight around the table and still more packages under the tree. Jim, the wine snob, would bring his traditional magnum of really good champagne and an assortment of other wines. Andrew would bring an arrangement of flowers for the table and later, the gift of his music for all to enjoy.

Olympia's two sons, Randall and Malcolm, now fully grown and on their own, would celebrate the day with their spouses' families but would join them tomorrow for Boxing Day. Her daughter Laura and her wife Gerry were expecting a baby boy in late winter and planned to stay in California.

Olympia pondered all of this on the way back from the church and smiled. Life was good. Her pro-tem family would be waiting for her when she got home. There would be more presents under the tree and a glass of Jim's latest must-have wine waiting for her—that and more love than she'd ever known. The realist in her reminded her this was a day out of time, and there was still so much work to be done. The romantic in her suggested she stop thinking, shut the hell up, and enjoy the day.

Olympia staggered through the back door in a blast of icy wind with her arms wrapped around an enormous gourmet gift basket, compliments of the congregation. The kids were in the sitting room, playing with their new things, the cats were in hiding, and everyone else was buzzing around the kitchen. Emilio, somewhat overwhelmed by it all and still unsure of his position in the order of things, had positioned himself at the edge of the action. But even from the sideline, he was smiling and obviously enjoying himself. Olympia did wonder how he would react to seeing Jim and Andrew together. How many openly gay couples did he know? Did he know any? But she didn't have much time to think about that or anything else. Jim was already calling them all to the table.

The much-anticipated dinner turned out to be a lovely mélange of traditional American and English foods including Brazilian cheese breads made by Emilio and a special Jamaican dish made of rice and gungo peas from Andrew.

If this is my Christmas, thought Olympia, I'll take it. It was the first year that none of her kids were present, and she realized she was fine with it. They were happy and creating holiday traditions of their own now, as they should. Over the joyful noise of the multiple conversations around the table, she heard a contented little *bing* in the next room and raised her glass in grateful acknowledgement.

Each of them slithered off to where they'd hidden their own stash of family gifts and set them out under the tree. By mutual agreement, anything that went under the tree could not cost more than ten dollars, and less was better. This meant the gifts would be small, thoughtful, hand-made, a thrift-shop find, or something wonderfully silly.

"M'lords and ladies," bellowed Frederick for a second time that day, "much magic and merriment await us thither." He pointed grandly to the sitting room.

"What he say?" whispered Emilio into Andrea's ear. As the two newest members of the group, they stayed close.

"We are going into the next room for more presents," she responded. "Come on."

He didn't look convinced, but he did as he was told and followed the others into the sitting room. Under the tree was a new and much more varied collection of boxes and bags. As they were getting settled, Jim carried around a tray of after-dinner drinks: tiny, crystal goblets with sips of alcoholic ambrosia and two little glasses of fizzy orange juice for the girls. He'd selected them all himself and was in his glory serving them out to his friends. It was time for the magic to begin for a second time, or perhaps a third time that day. Olympia had lost count, and she didn't care. It was all wonderful.

34

The minimalist gift idea turned out to be a rousing success. The girls made and decorated gingerbread boys and girls for everyone. Frederick took advantage of the sale table at the bookstore and his employee discount and chose books as his gifts. Andrea, it turned out, was a knitter like Olympia. She'd started knitting scarves as soon as she knew she'd be spending the holiday with Olympia. For Frederick, she'd chosen a light blue, the color his eyes, and for Olympia, a soft green for the same reason. Given the lack of time between his arrival and Christmas Day, she presented Emilio with two skeins of yarn and a picture of the future scarf.

Andrew and Jim, both culinary perfectionists, combined their efforts to make platters of the most exquisite Christmas cookies Olympia had ever seen. These were individual works of art.

Later, as promised, Andrew would play Olympia's recently acquired piano. Someone at the church had been getting rid of it, and Olympia was the first in line. She'd played the piano as a child and was still trying to remember where her fingers went. So it would be Andrew who would do the honors when it came time to sing Christmas songs.

For her little gifts, Olympia had scoured the local thrift shops for unusual coffee mugs, each befitting its recipient, and filled them with little surprises—everything from gourmet herbal tea bags to a tiny bottle of lavender oil for Andrea, a set of jacks for one twin, and miniature checker board for the other.

This left Emilio. Olympia had offered to help him, and he'd politely declined, but he was not absenting himself from the fun. He was waiting for his moment.

Meanwhile, Frederick was clamoring to start the annual game of charades, which Olympia didn't especially love, but it was part of his English tradition, and he reveled in the madcap lunacy of it all. Seeing that Emilio had a basket of packages in his arms, she shushed Frederick and turned to Emilio.

"My turn?" he said with a shy smile. "I have some small things."

Courtesy of Frederick taking him to the restaurant, he had some jumping lobster toys for the girls and scented candles for everyone else. In keeping with the season, he'd wrapped each one in paper Christmas napkins and tied it with green garden twine.

"And if it is okay with you," he said softly, "I have something more."

They waited, wondering what in the world this man with so little, who was still learning the language, was going to do next.

"I would like to tell you a Christmas story from my country. If I had a guitar, I would play and sing a folk song for you. But I don't, so I will just tell the story if thas' okay?"

Frederick stood, and when he had everyone's attention, he clapped his hand to his forehead. "Oh, dear. I think I left the back door open. I'll be right back."

Olympia held up her hands in the I-give-up position. "Whatever."

He was back in a tic, carrying something wrapped in a black trash bag tied at the top with a big red ribbon. He walked across the room and handed it to Emilio. Looking completely mystified, Emilio slowly undid the ribbon and lifted a partially refurbished guitar out of the garbage bag.

"And just for the record, I didn't break the ten-dollar rule," said Frederick. "I found it at the Salvation Army store, and I did a little work on it. I'll tell you, though, you didn't give me much time. I remember, in the grocery store, you telling me that you played the guitar back in Brazil. This one was pretty scabby looking, but it still had strings, and I was able to get it working. I'll do a little more work on it now that the cat—or rather the guitar—is out of the bag."

Emilio was speechless with emotion and gratitude.

"I can' sing right now. Maybe later?" He was already picking at the strings and easing it into tune.

"Anytime you're ready, Emilio. It's yours to keep."

"Perhaps after we have our Christmas puddings," said Olympia.

But the lonely, homesick man didn't answer. He was off in another world. His fingers found their way to the sounds and the rhythms of his native land, his people, and his family, the stuff of his DNA and that of his little daughter.

Olympia herded the rest of them back to the table, leaving Emilio to make friends with his new/old guitar. "Come join us when you're ready."

He nodded vaguely, already lost in his music.

Andrew, a professional musician himself and a wash-ashore from the island of Jamaica, understood perfectly. He, too, was a man from another country, so alone and far away sometimes, but in the music, he could go back. In the music, he could remember. In the music, he could dream.

Later, when the kids, beyond exhausted, were poured into

bed and the overstuffed adults were sprawled around the sitting room, Andrew noodled around on the piano and Emilio backed him up. Then through an unspoken cue known only to musicians, Emilio took the lead and moved up and down the fret board through a number of riffs and modulations before handing it back to Andrew. The others, unwilling to break the spell, were content to listen…and perhaps to dream.

One by one, they said their good nights and went off to their beds, leaving Frederick and Olympia, side by side on the sofa, staring into the fire, content in the day and content in that marital silence that good friends who happen also be married know so well.

"Ya done good, lady," said Frederick, using his very best American accent.

Olympia smiled and leaned unto his encircling arm. Tomorrow was another day, and Emilio was still homeless. The murder of Andrea's husband remained unsolved, and soon after the holidays, Andrea and the kids would be looking for housing. Over and around all of this, the Reverend Doctor Olympia Brown was hatching a plan. Meanwhile, she had a more immediate plan involving the man sitting next to her, who was twisting around and pulling something out of his back pocket.

"What's that?"

"A little something for you."

"But we agreed to keep it simple, remember?"

He nodded. "This is very simple."

He handed her a crumpled envelope. "Open it, please."

She did as she was bidden and yipped. "Frederick! This is way   more   than   ten   dollars.   Oh,   my   God. What…how…when…"

"In April, right after Easter. I already checked with the church, and there's no problem with your taking the time. So tell me; do you like it?"

"Frederick, who wouldn't like a cruise to London on the Queen Mary Two but it's way out of our budget."

"Out of your budget, my dear, but as it turns out, not out of mine."

"Will you please stop talking in riddles?"

"As it turns out, I got an uptick on my pension from the UK two years ago and somebody forgot to write it down. A couple of weeks ago, unbeknownst to you, I got a retro-check that all but covers our passage and a few days after that in London. I'm thinking theater and museums and restaurants and cathedrals until we pass out from all that unadulterated hedonism, and then we fly home. Merry Christmas, my love."

Bing!

"Now then, good wife, let us betake ourselves to bed."

35

It was two days after Christmas, and life in the Brown, Watkins, Riggs, and Vieira household was beginning to fall into a semi-routine. Emilio was back to work full-time and rode with Frederick back and forth to Loring with his bike in the back of Frederick's truck. He'd arranged to work days until he found housing, but he used his bike to get around town before and after work.

With the men gone and the children fed, dressed, and off in the sitting room with their mother, Olympia sat by herself in the kitchen, getting ready to start her own day. She planned to take on the matter of the empty church parsonage. She whispered a quick prayer for strength and courage and tapped in the number for Franklin Bowen. She was a woman on a mission, and the conservative and well- intentioned church president had no idea what he was in for.

"Hi, Franklin. I hope you and Gregg had a nice Christmas. Actually, I'm calling you on church business. Really good business, I think. Do you have time to sit down with me in my office sometime this week? I have an idea that I want to talk over with someone I trust before I mention it to anyone else."

That alone was enough to set the man in motion.

Curiosity and flattery never failed. The compliment was not hollow. She did trust him. And curiosity opened many a locked door. It just so happened, he said, he did have some time that very afternoon. Would that be agreeable? *Is the Pope a Catholic?*

They agreed to meet at two in her office. This would give them ample time to talk and allow Olympia to get home before dark and hopefully before the predicted snow started to fall, whichever came first.

"It would be silly to pretend you haven't piqued my curiosity, Reverend. Can you give me a clue as to what you're thinking?"

"Pastoral silence?"

"Of course."

"I have had some further thoughts about the parsonage."

"Oh, come now. Is that all you're going to tell me?"

Olympia grinned like a Cheshire cat. "Yup."

"A woman of mystery."

"Right again."

Olympia pocketed the phone and set about tidying up the kitchen. Breakfast was a merry madness in a house with four adults, six-year-old twins, and two cats all sitting at and/or crawling around and under the kitchen table.

When she was satisfied the place would pass muster, if not close inspection, she poured herself a second cup of coffee. Before sitting down, she shooed the cats off the counter, encouraging their departure with a handful of treats. Now, she could begin to work out the details of her plan.

Her intent from the day she'd started as interim minister at the church was to shake things up, rattle more than a few cages, and in the long run, open a few crusty New England hearts. They weren't called God's frozen people for no reason. Olympia had her work cut out for her and then some. It was what she was called to do, and she loved it.

Andrea and the girls had agreed to begin some of the

post-Christmas clean-up in her absence as well as go snow-storm shopping for milk, bread, batteries, and junk food—in other words, the basics.

"I'll put something in the crock-pot for supper tonight, as well," she added. "Something vegetarian for the base, and then those who want to can add whatever I decide to make for a side."

Olympia smiled in gratitude. "I'll make the wine, beer, cocoa, and sugar run on the way home. My mother always said you can never have enough hot chocolate in a snowstorm."

Andrea lifted a bemused eyebrow. "Did your mother really say that?"

Olympia chuckled and shook her head. "Nope, I did."

"Thought so."

FRANKLIN BOWEN always bragged that you could set a clock by him, and he was right. At precisely two, he walked through the door. Olympia had gotten there early enough to make tea in the church's 1800s china pot and set out the matching cups and saucers. She made an arrangement of Christmas cookies on another porcelain church treasure and set it on the coffee table between them.

She poured the tea with ritual precision, offered him milk, honey and/or lemon to enhance it, and held out the plate of cookies. Then she adjusted and stirred her own cup.

Franklin was no fool. He too had played such stalling-for-time games.

"Okay, Reverend Lady, what, pray tell, is the object of this delightful exercise? You said you've been thinking about the parsonage. So tell me. Exactly what are you thinking about the parsonage?"

"In two words, short-term renting it. I know of a woman

in need of temporary housing, no more than a year, and likely much less. She is a pediatrician with two little girls, and she can afford market-value rent."

"She's the widow of the man who was killed here a couple of weeks ago."

"Right in one. She wants to get a place in town so she can keep the kids in school while she looks for a place to buy. I was wondering if I, or maybe we—" She stopped and flashed him a most winning smile. "Do you think we might approach the board with such a proposal?"

Franklin looked interested.

Thus encouraged, she continued. "We both know it is not good for a house to be unoccupied. It's a big house for only three people, but she doesn't have to use all of it. The way I see it, it's a win-win-win. The mother gets good safe housing at a fair price, and the church is not supporting an empty building and worrying about the heat cutting out the way it did here at the church."

"That's two wins. What's the third?"

"The church gets to practice what it purports to preach. It opens its doors and arms to a person in need."

"Is this woman a member of the church?"

"Would that make a difference?"

"It would to some."

"Would it make a difference to you?"

He had to stop and think about his response to that one, but he finally said, "No, probably not, but I repeat, it might be to some of the others."

"If I have your support, I think we can probably bring them along. It will cost us nothing to do a good deed, and we make money in the bargain."

"You make it sound like an offer I can't refuse."

"Something like that."

In the end, it didn't take much more convincing. Olympia had done her homework, but she almost lost it when Franklin stopped, cleared his throat, and carefully asked, "I, uh, well, and don't get me wrong when I say this, but I'm assuming this is a Caucasian family…"

"And if it isn't?"

He held up his hand to stop the firestorm. "Relax, Reverend. If they aren't, it might make it a harder sell to some of us, but I like the idea, and I'll support you."

"She's white. She's fallen on some hard times, and she needs help. You in?"

There was no hesitation this time. "Of course I am."

She breathed a silent sight of relief. *One down and one to go.* That second one, a place for Emilio, she would save for later. She hoped the surprise factor would work in her favor. It had in the past.

36

O nce he was on board with the idea, Franklin wasted no time in setting up a meeting of the Parish Committee. Because it was the quiet week between Christmas and the New Year, people's schedules were more relaxed. They would meet at ten in the morning, on the upcoming Friday. Olympia was ready and armed for bear.

The snow that had fallen earlier in the week had transformed Loring into a New-England-themed Christmas card, and Olympia needed her sunglasses to get to work that morning.

By quarter after ten, the seven board members were seated on borrowed chairs in a lopsided circle in Olympia's office. She'd set out coffee, tea, and the remains of the Christmas cookies on the coffee table. Franklin wasted no time.

"Good morning everyone, and thank you for coming. The reverend has approached me with an idea concerning a use for the temporarily empty parsonage. I listened, and when she finished, I told her I was positively inclined but that we should bring it before the board for full consideration and debate."

Curious looks and affirmative nods. Church governing

boards could be the best allies or worst enemies. Consulting them, asking their advice and guidance, and listening to their responses go a long way in building a strong and positive relationship. The same could be said about marriages, and Olympia often did when counseling a pre-nuptial couple. Olympia was cautiously encouraged.

"Reverend Olympia, why don't you explain it?" said Bowen. "Thank you, Franklin, and thank you all for coming on such short notice. I'm pretty sure none of you know this, but a couple of weeks before Christmas, a woman came into my office with her twin daughters in need of help and sanctuary. A safe place. I didn't know it then, but within days, she would become a widow. She is the wife of the doctor who was murdered here in town."

A chorus of astonished and sympathetic gasps.

"Because of the immediate need and the confidential nature of her situation, I took her and the children home with me, and they have been there ever since. I haven't said anything to her as yet because I thought it only fair to approach you all before I did."

Lots of positive nods and affirmative comments.

"She's doing well and wants to come back and live here in town so the children can return to school, and they all can get back to some sort of a normal life."

"I can see where this is going," said Harry Reynolds, one of the younger members of the congregation. "And I think I'm going to like it, but my question is, if we say yes, how long would she stay? I mean, we're going to need that parsonage for the next minister. What then?"

"I'm getting to that," said Olympia.

She outlined her plan, assuring them that it was short-term. She explained the woman would be looking for a new home as soon as the investigation was settled enough for her to dispose of the house where the murder took place.

When she finished, the questions and the challenges flew

through the air and around the room like a hive of anxious bees, ready to sting if aggravated and just as ready to make honey if soothed and properly treated. In the end, they made honey. But it took them through most of the morning and the assurance that it was temporary, for the committee to finally give it the go-ahead and take it before the entire congregation for final approval.

After the vote, the one stalwart hold-out, Harry Reynolds, asked if they might consider housing her in the apartment over the garage instead of taking up the whole house. His argument was that, since it was only a single mother with two kids, they could manage just as well in the smaller space, and it would be easier all around.

"Easier for what?" Olympia growled under her breath. Up a flight of stairs with groceries for three, a single bedroom, a Barbie-sized bathroom and kitchen. No way!

Olympia withheld her angry response with some difficulty. She slowly and carefully restated her reasons why a woman who has just been through hell, who plans to start coming to this church with her children, and who will soon open a pediatric practice in town, should be given the lesser of two choices? "And furthermore," she added, "shouldn't a church which has a proud history of sheltering people from harm, continue to honor that history by continuing it into the present day?"

Responding to the circle of frowns and dark looks, Reynolds demurred, muttering, "Well, as long as it's temporary. I guess I can go along with it."

She thanked him and all of them then held up her right index finger. "Hold on, good people. If you can give me another ten minutes, I have one more thing for you to consider before we adjourn. And interestingly enough, Harry, it concerns the very space you were talking about for some of the very same reasons."

Franklin Bowen had been caught off guard, and it was

clear he didn't like it. She was taking a big risk, and she knew it, but she also knew that, in all fairness, by presenting it to everyone all at once, no one could ever accuse her of stacking the deck. Conversely, if she'd said anything to Franklin beforehand and he was opposed to the idea, she never would have gotten onto the table. Well, here goes, she thought. Double or nothing.

The tension in the room was rising, and so was Olympia's blood pressure. "Do you remember the Brazilian man who fell ill here also a couple of weeks before Christmas?"

They did.

Carefully omitting the part about his living in the church basement, she stated her case. "Well, when I visited him in the hospital, I learned where and how he was living before he got sick. I invited him to come and stay with Frederick and me while he recovers. He's still with us, but he needs a place of his own. So I am suggesting we offer him the garage apartment…and we offer it to him free of charge for a specified period of time, say two or three months while he gets back on his feet. Then we have another conversation about a more permanent arrangement. We have just voted to offer sanctuary and safe haven to the widow of a murder victim. I am asking you to stretch yourselves and your generosity a little further and give a homeless Brazilian man the same courtesy and consideration."

"Does he have a green card?"

"No, he does not."

And then the spit hit the fan.

The questions and accusations ran the gamut from kindly asking after the man's health, and did he have a family, and was he going to apply for citizenship to who did she think she was anyway, telling them what to do? One red-faced church member went as far as to accuse her of being a temporary fill-in who didn't understand their ways and was trying to shove her do-gooder liberal ideas down their throats.

Olympia stood her ground, and when the first wave of anger and unrest subsided, she addressed them again, this time, telling his personal story. She told them that, in Brazil, he'd been a history teacher in a small college. She told them about the loss of his wife and the baby daughter in Brazil he hadn't seen in almost a year. She told them about his working himself to the point of exhaustion to send them money and his dream of one day, bringing them here. They were beginning to listen, and more importantly, Olympia realized they were beginning to hear what she was saying.

"So where was he living before he got sick? He had to be living somewhere. Why can't he just go back there?" asked Harry Reynolds.

It was the question she'd been waiting for.

"He could, but I don't think any of you would want to see that happen—for insurance purposes, if nothing else."

She had them now. Arousing curiosity was the best way in the world to get someone to listen to you. She'd done it before, and she was doing it again.

"So where was he living?"

"He was camping out in a forgotten crawl space underneath an unused staircase in the cellar of a public building. He'd slip in at night, use the bathrooms, charge his phone, and get back on the streets before anyone came in to work." Olympia began to enjoy this, and as she continued the story, she saw the light beginning to dawn across Franklin's forehead. He smiled.

She flicked him a don't-say-anything look and continued with her story. She was on a roll now. "Before he got sick, he'd sometimes come to services here. In fact, I think many if not most of you would probably recognize him if you saw him. He's come to coffee hour on occasion."

"Emilio!"

Olympia nodded. "That's him. And I think that because this place and these people were somewhat familiar to him and have been kind to him, he made the wise choice of coming here to collapse, rather than on the street or a gas station bathroom."

They were all nodding in agreement now, even Reynolds.

"The man stumbled upstairs seeking help because he was living downstairs in our own dirt cellar."

Gasps and outraged noises.

"He's been sleeping in the Indian closet which, as you all know, became a slave closet, a place where people were hidden for safety and protection. Emilio Vieira came here for sanctuary, and he found it, only we didn't know we were offering it.

"Right now, he's living with Frederick and me. He's welcome, and he's safe, and he can stay as long as he needs to. But this man has a dream, and I'm asking this church to make it part of your mission of helping the less fortunate to help this man realize his dream. I'm asking you to consider letting him have the garage apartment for free or perhaps in return for some custodial work on the church property." She paused, gathering steam. "And I'm also asking you to consider sponsoring him so he can apply for that green card and eventually apply, legally, for US citizenship."

She waited, letting her words hover in the air around them. "Emilio doesn't have a home. His family is several thousand miles away, and he wants a better life for himself and his baby. I believe we can do something about that if we choose to. If we choose to welcome the stranger, comfort those in need, and in the end, practice what we purport to preach as members of this church."

She paused to let all of that sink in. "I am not asking for a decision right now. This is going to take some hard thinking and likely some difficult conversations. I am asking you to please go home and simply ponder this, and then perhaps, early next week, we can have another meeting to discuss it.

"Meanwhile, you need to know that Andrea, her children,

and Emilio are all safe and secure and welcome to continue living in my home for as long as they want. We have the room. That means, despite my request, and my obvious preference, there is no pressure on this congregation either way. I do feel compelled to ask, and I am compelled to abide by your decision."

She pressed her two palms together and held them to her chest. "Thank you all for hearing me out. Not everyone would give me that opportunity."

"Thank you, Reverend," said Franklin. "You've certainly given us some food for thought."

"I can only hope it doesn't give you indigestion." She smiled, and they sort of smiled back. "I think it's time to go home."

37

As the others stayed back to clean up, Harry Reynolds followed Olympia out into the parking lot. "Have you got a minute, Reverend?"

"Of course."

"I owe you an apology."

She tried to wave it away, but he insisted.

"I was pretty nasty a few minutes ago. I guess I felt blind-sided or something. Anyway, I called you a crappy name, and I'm sorry I did. Will you forgive me?" He held out his hand, and Olympia took it.

"No apologies necessary. It got heated. Sometimes, we say things we don't mean."

"Oh, I meant it when I said it, but you've convinced me otherwise. Way otherwise. I just want you to know that I think I can help. One of my best friends is an immigration lawyer. I'm going to get in touch with him the minute I get home."

Olympia held on to his hand, blinking back the tears of gratitude. "Oh, Harry, you've just given me the best Christmas present of my entire life. I mean it. Thank you."

"Don't mention it, at least until we get things moving. Just don't mention it."

Olympia smiled and held a finger to her lips. She'd heard him use we. He was on her side.

She wisely waited until she got into the car before waving her arms in the air and yelling, "Thank you, Jesus. Merry Christmas, Happy Chanukah, Hallelujah, Happy New Year, Happy Groundhog Day, and happy whatever else you've got up your sleeve, God! It's one down and one to go, and I'm in for the long haul."

Inside the church, the members of the board had not put on their coats and their hats and followed Olympia out of the church. By a unanimous vote, they reconvened the meeting in executive session.

38

"So, ladies and gentleman, I would say we have a bit of a problem here."

"I think the problem is the minister." Dennis Wolf crossed his arms fiercely and protectively across his barrel chest. "She's crossed the line this time. What we do with our property is none of her goddamn business. We've been here for three hundred years without someone telling us what we should do. Who the hell does she think she is to tell us to take in some guy who squats free of charge in the church cellar and rides around town on a bicycle? We don't know anything about him. He could be an ISIS terrorist for all we know."

"Do you say that because he has brown skin?" Franklin's color was beginning to rise.

"I say that because we don't know anything about him. The woman with the two kids, well I can see that. She already lives here in town, and it would be temporary. I say charity begins at home. Besides, she's going to pay some rent. What's he going to give us besides a liability? There're women and children who come to this church. We need to protect them."

Lesley Pitts, a long-time member, stood up to speak. "I cannot believe I'm hearing this. This sounds like everything we oppose. Meeting in secret. Protect the women and children from the dark stranger even though you don't really know him. Never mind that our own minister has him living in her own home with that woman and two little children. Never mind that the man came to our church in need of help and sanctuary. What are we turning into? It's not our minister that's the problem here; it's us."

Dennis was up and out of his chair. "Well, in my opinion, she's not a real minister. She's just a temporary... and if you go forward with this, I'll leave the church."

"I hope it doesn't come to that, but if it does, it will be your choice." Bowen paused, directing his words now to everyone, and not just to Dennis. "You know, my friends, conflict can destroy a relationship, or worked through, it can make it stronger. Clearly, we have some pretty intense feelings on both sides of this, and I think we should be able to express those feelings without fear or condemnation. Respect for divergent views is a cornerstone of our congregation. Picking up your marbles and going home is not how to grow and remain in community."

Wolf glared at him but remained in the room.

"As president of this congregation, I'm going to ask us all to stop, to step back from the brink and think. Think about what we value. Think about what we espouse, and think about how we intend to live out our values. And then we can have another meeting." He held up a warning hand. "May I remind you this meeting was in executive session, meaning it's confidential. It's important to keep it that way right now. More specifically, I am asking you not to start an email war over this. This is our issue. If we approve of the idea, we agree only to bring it before the entire congregation for the final vote. We do not make the decision. That's what makes us a congregational polity and not a top-down hierarchy."

This was greeted by a general mumbling and eventually, agreement.

BY NOW, the occupants of the Brown-Watkins household and extended pro-tem family seemed to have found their rhythm. They'd worked out an equitable rotation of chores: cooking, clean-up, housework, and transportation. On a couple of occasions, Andrea offered to drive Emilio to work with the understanding that Frederick would bring him home.

The girls, however, were getting restless. The newness and sense of adventure had worn off, and they were missing their friends and ready to go back to school. By now, they understood they would not see their father again, and the questions about why this was so were less frequent.

Olympia had told no one other than Frederick about her plans for the future occupancy of the parsonage. No point in tempting fate or setting Andrea and Emilio up for an unpleasant disappointment. They'd been through too much already.

Now, as she signaled and turned onto her street, she felt pretty good. She had two heavy hitters on her side in this. But she knew there were some equally opinionated people on the other side. She suspected Andrea and the girls would be given the go-ahead. But what about Emilio? If they said yes to one and not to the other, how would she feel? Would she even be able to continue on as the minister? On the other hand, could she walk away from it and them if they decided in their own wisdom to deny sanctuary to Emilio? That's what it was all about, really. Sanctuary. Safe place. Protection from harm. Other churches and cities around the country were struggling with this issue as well. Fear of the other is instinctive. So is wanting to help and share of one's bounty. Mostly.

Wittingly or unwittingly, it was possible she'd put herself into the same situation she'd just thrust upon the governing board of the church: my way or the highway.

If they refused to offer Emilio sanctuary, could she or

would she be able to stay on as their minister? But if she left, was leaving the same as throwing in the towel and abandoning her own principles? Emilio did have a place to live, but it was away from his work. He could get another job in or close to Brookfields. No, it wasn't about a place to live or another job. It was bigger than that. Did these people believe in welcoming the stranger, or did they not? It was the principle of the thing, and if nothing else, Olympia was a woman of principle. Dammit!

She turned off the engine and sat in the rapidly cooling car and pondered her situation. In the rearview mirror, she saw a white car slow down and then speed up as it drove past the end of the drive. Must be somebody looking for a house number, she thought, and promptly dismissed it and continued with her ruminations.

The whole housing thing was out of her hands, but it was all her doing, wasn't it? She'd set the gears in motion. Jim would tell her, once again, not to get so involved in other people's business, knowing full well his words would have no effect whatsoever. Frederick would roll his eyes and then step right up to the plate and do whatever was needed. God, she loved that man!

"What will be, will be," she said aloud, her breath making little white puffs in the now freezing car. It would go one way or the other, and then it would be decision-making time for her. She shivered. Time to go in.

"WHAT HO, MY LOVE?" Frederick stood in the kitchen, holding the teapot in one hand and a wine glass in the other. "Pick your poison."

Olympia looked at her watch. Although she didn't really adhere to the no drinks before five in the afternoon rule, it was still a bit early. Or was it?

"I'll have some wine—just a half glass—and a cup of tea as well, please."

"Been a long day, has it?"

"And it's not over yet."

"So I take it they didn't jump at the idea of renting out the parsonage?"

"More like they danced around the edges. It's a lot for them to think about."

"What are the chances?" He held out her wine and set about making the tea.

"I'm pretty sure they'll say yes to Andrea."

"But not Emilio?"

She shook her head. "No idea. It's going to be a real stretch for them. I just hope they don't snap in the process."

LATER THAT EVENING, in Loring by the Sea, the white SUV drove slowly down the street and passed the house where the murder took place. Now, two days later, it was back, this time parked two blocks away from the crime scene. White SUVs are a common sight in affluent areas where soccer moms drive their children all over town, so anyone seeing it wouldn't give it a second thought. If anyone did bother to look, they would have seen a man in a hoodie sitting behind the wheel, watching for something in the rearview mirror. If that same someone was really paying attention, he or she would have seen a second man, dressed in dark clothing, approach the vehicle from behind and slip into the passenger seat. But in the dark of winter, on a cold night in January, who is looking out the window counting cars? The two men in the white SUV depended on that. They knew their business.

OLYMPIA DIDN'T EXPECT the call asking her to come and "have a conversation" about the "parsonage usage issue" as soon as it did. Whenever she was asked to have a conversation about something, it did not usually bode well. In a flat voice, Franklin asked when she might be available for a meeting with the board.

"Not good, I take it," said Olympia.

"I'm afraid not."

"I can be there this afternoon or any time tomorrow. The sooner the better, right? I know it's confidential, but can you give me a clue? I'd rather not be blindsided."

"It was a four-three split. Yes to her, no to him."

"Damn."

"I'm sorry."

"It's not your fault."

"I know, but I don't like how this is going down."

"That bad, eh?"

"It got pretty ugly. If I were you, I'd bring a good-sized umbrella with you when you come, because I have the feeling a whole lot of crap is going to hit the fan, and I don't want it sticking to you if I can help it."

"Thanks for the heads up, my friend. Knowing I have you on my side counts for a lot, you know."

"That and a dollar fifty may or may not get you a cup of coffee. I'll do a call around and get right back to you."

Olympia ended the call and spat out, "Damn-hell-shit."

"You called?" said Frederick.

Within ten minutes, Franklin rang back to say the meeting had been called for two that afternoon. Happy New Year, thought Olympia. The perfect way to close out the old year and begin the new. What was it about churches?

JANUARY 1866

We are <u>not</u> enjoying the annual January thaw. Everything that was frozen or snow-covered is melting, and the roads are rivers of ice and mud. The children are restless and want to be outside, but cleaning them up afterward is too much effort. Even Sammy the cat will not go out except for the most pressing of needs.

I digress. With the holidays behind us I must come to terms with what I shall do next. The house in Cambridge weighs heavily on me. It is a lovely home, but I cannot live in two places any longer and will put it up for sale. I am happier in the country with a garden and trees, and on an east wind, the sweet scent of the ocean.

But more to the point, Susan, Nathan, and I have learned the full and tragic extent of Lottie's perpetual melancholy. The poor woman has a child, a daughter, who was taken from her and sold because the child too closely resembled the child's father, the man who forced himself upon her, and wanted to hide his most grievous transgression…her master.

More Anon… LFW

39

Olympia gave herself the advantage by getting to the church before everyone else. She would be the one to open the door and invite them into the building. In general, this was a very social and chatty congregation. They liked each other, and they liked to do things together. Today, the people who stood at the door were quiet. Some openly scowled in Olympia's direction while others stared at the floor. Franklin Bowen and Harry Reynolds, her two allies, looked distinctly uncomfortable. Seven board members and Olympia... She suspected the other yes vote was probably Lesley Pitts, but she couldn't be sure.

When they were assembled, Franklin thanked them all for coming on such short notice, cleared his throat more often than necessary, and called the meeting to order. "Reverend Brown, the board met for a second time in executive session to discuss your proposition for the temporary use of the parsonage and the garage apartment, and we reached a yes and no decision. The board decided to allow Andrea Riggs and her children to occupy the parsonage on a short-term, temporary basis while she looks for permanent housing in

Loring. The board has decided against allowing Emilio Vieira to occupy the garage apartment."

"I see," said Olympia. "Can you tell me how the board came to this decision? I need to know for myself, and both Andrea and Emilio deserve to know why one drew the lucky straw, and one will have to keep on looking."

"You haven't said anything to them, have you?" asked Franklin.

"No, but the subject will certainly come up."

"Board meetings are confidential. Members can't divulge what goes on in a closed meeting."

"I am not a member of the board. I sit, ex-officio at meetings when invited. I am allowed to cast opinions, not votes. I'm not going to say anything, but we all know that, one way or another, people are going to know."

Dennis Wolf leaned forward in his chair. Wolf by name and wolf by nature. "Look, Reverend. You're a minister, and you see the best in everyone. You're supposed to. We understand that, but we have been a congregation in Loring for over three hundred years. This church will be here long after we are all gone. We have to think about the image we project. It's all well and good to welcome the stranger, and I think we have. But it's an entirely different matter to take him in to live with us. Emilio comes to church when he feels like it. He has coffee with us when he wants to, and to be honest, he's welcome to come back again. Hell, we can even try and find him a place to live. That would be a good thing for the church to do. Don't you think?"

"I think it's a token gesture. Well meant, no doubt, and I appreciate that, but Emilio doesn't need a place to live. He has one. He's living with my husband and me in our house. So are Andrea and her children. And if your decision is to say yes to one and no to the other, I'd rather they continued to live with me than have to tell Emilio that the church he came to seeking sanctuary has refused his request."

"Wait a goddamn minute here...Reverend. You make us sound like mean-spirited, narrow-minded stinkers. We're not. We're just being careful. This man is breaking the law. He's here illegally, and he's sponging off the state. If he was doing this the right way, it would be different, but he's not. We don't owe him anything. If we let him live here, we'll be breaking the law by harboring a fugitive from justice."

"You are absolutely right." Olympia's face flushed, and her voice rose. "You owe him nothing. I'll be sure I tell him that. Emilio, the church I work for owes you nothing. So you can stay home with us until somebody tips off the immigration police and they can catch you and then deport you."

"Nice, Reverend. Really nice...for a temporary fill-in, which is what you are, you really have a way with words. Maybe we'll take this up again when we have a real minister. Meanwhile, we made a decision, and you lost." Dennis had flushed a dark red, and he began to sweat.

Franklin was on his feet, with his arms outstretched. "Stop it! Listen to yourselves. We are a church, for God's sake, not the U.S. Congress or a cat-and-dog fight. The reverend made a proposal that you voted down. She's upset, I'm upset, and two others of us are upset, but this is how we do business. Now we live with it."

Olympia held up her hand. "Requesting permission to apologize. I lost my head, and I lost control of my mouth, and I'm sorry I did. Good things don't happen that way. I only made it worse. Let's just leave it that Emilio and Andrea will continue to stay on with me. And having said that, it would be wonderful if the church could help both of them find housing they can afford. That way, you folks don't have to stretch further than you feel able to do right now. At the same time, you will be actively helping two good people find decent housing. It's not really offering them sanctuary. It's a middle path, but it is a path forward. How do you feel about that?"

The tension in the room dropped to a breathable level. In

that suggestion, she had given them a graceful way out and a doable way forward.

"What do you think, folks?" asked Franklin.

"It's worth considering," said Bill Christmann, one of the more reasonable members of the board. "I like it, but I need to think about it. When's the next scheduled board meeting?"

"Second Tuesday."

"That's time enough."

Tom Cummiskey, who had not spoken before, looked shamefaced and embarrassed. "Don't be angry with us, Reverend. It's seems we're more stuck in our ways than I thought we were. These things take time."

"Naming the problem is the first step," said Olympia. "It doesn't get any easier after that, but at least you know what you're dealing with."

"Move to adjourn the meeting," said Franklin.

"So moved."

40

B y mid-January, the murder of Dr. James Cabot was still under investigation, but the two most immediate suspects in the murder had been cleared and were getting on with their lives.

Andrea and the children had moved into the parsonage. After hours of impassioned/heated/high-decibel discussion at the church, Emilio had been granted temporary space and asylum in in the garage apartment. The girls were back in school, and Andrea was looking into setting up a practice.

Emilio, still living under the immigration radar, was working with a pro-bono lawyer and exploring options. His manager made him full-time at the restaurant, and as long as the snow wasn't too deep, he regularly rode his bike to work. If she had time, Andrea would give him a lift, and if he was home during the day, he would look after the kids when they came home from school if their mother was out.

The final and hard-won agreement with the church was that Andrea could live there for a year or until such time as she found a place of her own. She would, by her own choice, start coming to church with her children. No one, least of all Olympia, had made that a condition of occupancy. Emilio could stay until such time as the church had need of the space, which, they assured him, was not very likely.

With the parsonage already partially furnished, Andrea had little to do in terms of furniture moving. And when she did need something, she could get it from the other house, which would soon be on the market. If it sold before she had a new place, she would put everything in storage. The light at the end of the tunnel was getting brighter, and Dr. Andrea Riggs was moving steadily and more confidently toward it.

It was just past nine o'clock, and the children were in bed and well asleep. Andrea was half watching TV and half drowsing over a dull book when the doorbell rang. She wasn't expecting anyone. She didn't really have any friends yet, not ones who would come by at nine at night without calling first. Emilio? Olympia? Someone from the church?

She put down the book, walked out into the marble-tiled foyer of the grand old house, and opened the door. A man in a black hoodie holding a gun pushed past her and walked into the house.

"Shut-up, and do what I say. Scream and I'll shoot."

"What do you want?"

"I said shut up."

He gestured with his gun. "Get your coat. You're coming with me. Now." He pointed to the umbrella stand by the door. "And drop your cell phone in there."

"I'm not going anywhere. I can't. My...." She caught herself in time. Whatever happened, she would not mention her sleeping children.

"You're gonna do what you're told, lady. I killed your husband, and I have no problems killing you. I don't like shooting women and children, but I will if you make me."

Andrea shook so violently she could barely talk. "What do you want?" She clutched her arms and held them tightly against her body in an attempt to stop the trembling, but it wasn't working. She was terrified, and she was freezing. The gunman had not bothered to shut the door behind him.

"Your husband tried to fuck with us. He backed out of a big deal, and he paid the price. We're pretty sure he was dealing on the side, and we think there's still a pile of drugs at the house. You lived with him. We figure you have to know where it is or at least where to start looking. We know the cops didn't find anything when they searched the place, so my guess is they are still there, and you're gonna help me find them. So stop shaking, and get your fucking coat."

Andrea was trapped, and she knew it. She pulled on her coat and started to reach for her purse.

The man barked and waved his gun. "The cell phone. Dump it. Get a move on, will you. I'm runnin' out of patience."

Wordlessly, Andrea did as she was told.

"Now, walk out the door."

"I have to lock the door."

"Oh, for Christ's sake." But the man in the hoodie did stop outside the door and let her do it.

"Walk over to the white car, get into the front seat, and don't try anything funny."

"Don't worry." At that point, Andrea had run out of options, and much as she hated leaving the children alone, by doing as she was told, she was trying to keep them safe. As a rule, they slept through the night without waking. And if they did wake up and she was not there, she hoped they would know to call Emilio. She started walking slowly toward the car, intent only on keeping her children—and hopefully herself—alive.

No one saw him standing in the shadows watching and listening to the entire heart-stopping drama. He'd been riding his bike home from work when he saw Andrea's door standing open. She didn't leave doors open. Something was wrong. His months living on the street had taught him how to spot trouble. He got off his bike, slipped behind a tree, and listened. From the way the man in the doorway stood, Emilio instinctively knew he was holding a gun, and he was pointing it at Andrea. Having a gun changed all the rules. If he rushed in now, he would risk her life, and possibly his own. And what about the twins? Emilio had come to love those little girls.

He waited.

Life on the streets had taught him when to wait, when to move like a cat on silent feet, and when to come in for the kill.

He waited.

Andrea walked like a broken robot to the passenger door of the SUV and reached for the handle.

"Hold it," snarled the gunman. "Stop right there. Turn around."

"God help me," she whispered.

She stopped, turned, and watched Emilio leap like a panther out of the shadows and smash a garden planter onto the gunman's head, dropping him like a stone onto the sidewalk at their feet.

"You go call police. I sit on him 'til they come. It's okay. I got the gun."

Andrea sucked in a gulp of cold fresh air and then ran back to the door and fumbled for the key before finally pulling open the door. Once inside, she grabbed her phone out of the umbrella stand and called 911.

"Please don't use the siren," she begged. "My children are asleep, and I don't want to frighten then. The bad man is unconscious, and a good man is sitting on top of him. He's not going anywhere."

Together, they waited. Emilio sat on top of the prone gunman, and Andrea clung to a fencepost for support. Distraught as she was, her only thought was not thank God she was safe, but worry that Emilio would be questioned and deported. She saw a police car approaching, lights flashing, but no siren, and watched as it pulled up behind the SUV. The man on the ground began to stir. Emilio growled something in Portuguese and hung on like an octopus. And then it was over.

The police took charge, first getting the now semi-conscious, bloody man into a seated position and checking him over. Emilio handed them the man's gun then moved back out of the way. Andrea, her strength returning fast, stepped forward to do the talking. All of the talking.

In the end, with the assailant in handcuffs and in back of the squad car, the officers took both of their names, thanked Emilio for his bravery and quick action, and said they would like to take statements from both of them. But, they added, it could wait until tomorrow.

THE NEXT MORNING, as the girls worked their way through their Cheerios, Andrea casually asked how they were feeling that morning and if they'd slept well.

"Uh-huh," said Julianne, her mouth full of food.

"I thought I heard the phone ring," said Marybeth. "Maybe I be dreaming." She still got her words a little wrong once in a while. Andrea, smiled. They would be little for such a short time, and she was actively cherishing every precious moment. She'd lost so many. Never again.

And then there was Emilio. How do you say thank you to a man who saved your life? Then, it came to her.

First, she needed to call Olympia and tell her what had happened—that her husband's killer had been found and apprehended and she'd survived yet another life-threatening crisis. After that, she'd call her lawyer, and after that, a realtor. But first things first. Finish breakfast, get the kids off to school, and then sit and stare at the wall for a couple of hours. The beds and the dishes could wait. Now, she could really start putting the pieces of life and herself back together. The worst was over, and she'd made it through to a new day.

NEXT DOOR in his efficiency apartment, Emilio was finishing his own breakfast, and like Andrea, considering his options. The arresting officers had taken basic information, commended him for his bravery, and said they would be back in touch. But now what? He'd been working with the immigration lawyer recommended to him through Harry Reynolds. And while his choices were limited, now at least he had choices, when before he'd had none. Most of the options involved leaving the country and reapplying for entry and were pretty high-risk and expensive. He could continue as he was, staying on as an undocumented resident, but that meant living in the shadows and in constant fear of an ICE raid and capture. Probably the most promising idea was to apply for a work visa and get out of the restaurant, back into the classroom, and after that, behind his guitar in a jazz bar somewhere. Emilio blinked and shook his head. His dream was getting out of hand. Maybe he should sit down and talk with Frederick and Olympia. Frederick had a permanent green card. He'd been through the process. Maybe he'd have some ideas?

41

A few days after the murderer's arrest, Emilio was awakened by the sound of his cell phone. He'd dozed off in front of the TV. What riches, he thought, still not fully believing it. Two months ago, he was living in a dirt cellar in a space that was half the size of his present bathroom with nothing but his cell phone and a few borrowed books.

Another more insistent *brrrrrrrp brrrrrrrrrrrrrrrrrp* brought him out of his reverie. He picked up and hit the green button.

"This is Emilio."

It was his next-door neighbor. "Emilio, I wonder if you would like to come over and have dinner with us tonight or tomorrow night ....or sometime soon. I never said a real thank-you for what you did the other night. You saved my..." Her voice caught.

"You don have to thank me, Andrea. Tha was a very bad man. I wanted to kill him for hurting you, but I know better. Tha's alright."

"No really, I haven't cooked a big meal since Christmas dinner. I like to cook, and I like to have people to cook for. Now it's just me and the girls, so I don't often do anything fancy."

"I have to work tonight."

"So how about tomorrow?"

"Okay. I can bring wine from the restaurant. They give me a good price."

Andrea laughed. "Don't you understand? I am saying thank you to you. You don't have to bring anything. Besides, the girls totally love you. You tell them the best stories. They've been missing that, but I told them they couldn't pester you."

"What is pester mean?"

She paused, looking for the words. "It means, take too much of your time."

"Andrea, I have a little girl I can't tell stories to right now. They don pester me. I'll come tell them stories."

"But have dinner with us first?"

"I bring some wine."

Andrea smiled, knowing that a man— most men—never wanted to feel beholden. "You bring wine. I usually feed the girls at about six, so you can come next door any time after five."

"I can help you with the cooking."

"You can pour the wine and tell stories to the girls."

He laughed. "Yes, mama."

I'm not your mother, thought Andrea with a warm smile he had no way of seeing.

AT BOSTON POLICE HEADQUARTERS, Loring detectives English and Licowski were meeting with BPD detectives Lawrence and Lim. The four were crossing the final T's and dotting the remaining I's on part one of the Cabot murder case: the murder itself. They had the killer, they had the weapon, and they had the motive: a drug deal gone badly wrong. But the murder was a very small part, collateral damage, really, of a much larger investigation: a prescription drug operation that appeared to be connected to several Boston hospitals and likely far beyond those.

"Okay, so we've got this one about buttoned up, but the drug thing is still ongoing."

"Not our job, man," quipped Lawrence. "We do murder, robbery, and street crime. Special Investigations and the Drug Unit handle that stuff. Even crime is compartmentalized these days. Everybody's got a specialty."

"In this case, I think we got the easy side," said Lim. "I don't like drug people. They are nasty. They'll take out their own brother if he gets in their way or they think he's double-crossed them."

"Tell me about it," said Lawrence.

"That Brazilian guy deserves a medal, doesn't he? I mean he caught the killer, and he didn't even know it. He did our work for us."

"Emilio something or other?"

"Vieira," said English.

"That's it. I mean he took the guy out with a fucking flower pot. That's one for the books."

"Unbelievable, and you guys had him down for a prime suspect."

English held out his hands, palms up. "Well, of course. A brown-skinned man, a stranger, probably homeless, in a lily-white, pricey little seaside town. It's obvious, right?"

"I think you guys ought to do a little hard time here on the streets of Boston. Come see how the real people live. That kind of knee-jerk attitude really pisses me off."

"Hold on," said Detective Licowski, clearly on the defensive. "Whether or not we had him down as a suspect, which we didn't, it was the locals who called in the tips. We had to check it out. I don't like that crap either."

"They had the wife down as a person of interest as well. I couldn't really see her as a murderer, could you?"

"SOP— standard operating procedure. You know that. Always start with the next of kin," said English.

He nodded just as the desk-phone rang. "Lawrence here."

A pause.

"You're shitting me." He grabbed a piece of paper and started making notes. "Okay, we're on our way."

"What's up?" Lim, all business now, was already collecting her things.

"We got ourselves another dead doctor. Professional hit-job. They just pulled him out of the harbor over by the fish pier. The ME is on the way."

"How did they know it was a doctor?" asked English.

"Black guy, green scrubs, still had his wallet in his pocket. Everything in it; money, credit cards, hospital ID. Same hospital as Cabot. His name was Darnel Lincoln."

"Shit," said English.

"He was the man who came to us on the quiet and told us about Cabot's involvement with the drug business. That's when we called you. Damn. He said he was taking a risk in talking to us." Licowski shook her head in shock and disbelief. "I can't believe it. We never said who told us.""Somebody found out," said Esther Lim.

"This is bad."

"Life sucks and then you die," muttered English.

"Or you tell the truth and get shot."

"Come on, partner. We've got work to do," said Lim. And to Licowski and English she added, "We'll let you know what we find."

"He was a nice guy," said Licowski.

AT EXACTLY FIVE O'CLOCK, Emilio, now fully restored to health and holding a brown paper bag in which there could only be a bottle of wine, tapped on Andrea's back door. The girls, who knew he was coming for dinner, exploded into the kitchen and ran to greet him. He leaned down and gave each wiggling little girl a hug then held out the wine to Andrea.

"I don' know what you make, so I bring a Portuguese rosé. It's good with everything. It's the one my mother likes."

Andrea accepted the bottle and asked if she should put it into the fridge.

"It's cold already, but you can put it in the fridge, or out on the back step. It's cold out there too." To emphasize the fact, he rubbed his hands together and blew into them as if to warm them.

"Would you like something before dinner? A glass of beer, some water?"

"Tha's all right. I have some wine with the food."

"Okay then, you can stay here in the kitchen while I finish up, or you can go watch TV with the girls in the living room."

"If it's okay with you, I stay here. I like to sit in a kitchen with somebody cooking. I did that at home in Brazil. It smells good. What you making?"

"Well, I had to keep it pretty simple if I wanted the girls to eat any of it. I made spaghetti and meatballs for them and some salmon for us with a risotto Dijonaise with mushrooms and asparagus on the side."

"I know about salmon. It's a fish, and I know spaghetti, and I know risotto, but what is Dijonaise?"

"One of my favorites. It's something I make when I have somebody else to cook for. It's a mixture of Dijon mustard and mayonnaise that I stir into the rice. The girls don't really like it. It's yummy."

"Yummy?"

Andrea patted her stomach and smiled, an almost universal symbol for delicious.

"Now I understand." He smiled. Something he did much more often now.

"Is dinner ready yet?"

"Can Emilio tell us a story before supper?"

"You said when we moved we could get a dog. Is it time yet?"

"Can I have two meatballs?"

"Why don't we wait until afterwards to ask Emilio for a story? Dinner is almost ready. Girls, go wash your hands, then you can take him into the dining room and show him where to sit."

When they entered the dining room, Emilio saw a carefully set table and the three candles he had given them at Christmas.

"You wan me to light the candles?"

"That would be great, and here." She held out the wine and a book of matches. "Why don't you pour us some wine as well?"

"This is so nice, I'm not…" He looked down and gestured to his flannel shirt and jeans.

"Emilio, we are neighbors. I'm not dressed up either. I am wearing jeans too. I put out the candles because they are pretty, and you gave them to us."

"Okay." He paused then brightened. "Then I wash dishes for you. I am very good washing dishes." He grinned at her and spread his arms out to the side. "Many, many dishes."

"I'll dry." She pointed to the table. "But now, we eat."

THE MEAL WAS DELICIOUS. The conversation was relaxed, much the way it had been when they were still at Olympia's and the two of them would sit up after everyone went to bed just to enjoy the peace and quiet. Sometimes, they would chat. Sometimes, they would sit in companionable private silence. Over time, the two cautiously opened up to one another, and piece by jagged painful piece, they told their stories.

After dinner, after stories for the girls, after dishes, and after the kids were settled into bed, Emilio was collecting his things and making ready to leave.

"Don't go yet, Emilio." Andrea reached for the teakettle and held it up in his general direction. "How about a cup of tea before you go? It's nice having another adult around, and there's something I need to ask you."

"You ask, I do. You are very good to me."

"Wait until I ask before you say yes."

When the tea was made and poured, Emilio sat down at the kitchen table and waited while Andrea took the chair opposite him.

"What do you want me to do for you?"

"Actually, it's not so much for me, but it could help you."

He looked hopelessly confused.

"I think you should marry me."

Emilio slowly put down his teacup and looked across the table at Andrea.

"What you talking about?" He was wide-eyed.

"I'm serious. No romance, no responsibilities. We call it a marriage of convenience. If you were married to an American citizen, getting a resident card and eventually applying for citizenship would be so much easier. This is about a friend offering to help a friend...who saved her life."

"I..."He shook his head in disbelief.

"I am a widow. I can marry who I want, when I want. It would be strictly a business arrangement. You stay in your place. I stay in mine. Sometimes, we have dinner together or go for a walk. We're friends. We stay friends. Then, when you get legal status, we get a divorce, and you can bring your family here, maybe even get married again."

"But...you...I mean...I can't."

"Emilio, listen to me. You saved my life. That was a very bad man.

This is something I can do for you. You are a very good man. I want you to have your family with you. I can help you.

It will be legal and…" She paused. "It will cost one hell of a lot less than an immigration lawyer or going back and forth to Brazil for three or four years. A marriage in name only. It's not as if it's never been done before, and I'll bet anything that the good Reverend Olympia would be more than happy to help us."

Emilio was still speechless. Later, when Andrea related the story, she would say she was sure she saw the man's eyes revolving in opposite directions.

"Go home and think about it. Yes is fine. No is fine. If you say yes, it won't interfere with my life, and it won't interfere with yours. We are both free to do whatever we want. And if you find a nice lady to go out with, just don't tell her you're married, because once you're legal, you won't be. No one but us ever has to know."

"I have to go home now," said Emilio. "I think about this. You are a very good lady. My mother will love you."

"Think about it. There is no rush."

Emilio pulled on his jacket, and tucked the scarf that Andrea had since finished inside the collar and high around his chin. He crossed the kitchen, took her hand in his and kissed the back of it.

"*Obrigado, Senora*. Thank you, Mrs. Andrea. I go home and think."

42

L ate into that night, two people were separately deep in thought. The doctor was not having second thoughts about what she'd offered Emilio. She was mentally constructing her new practice. A marriage to Emilio would not affect her professional plans in the least. Tonight, it was the color scheme; calming colors for anxious children and parents but still welcoming and inviting. Shades of pink, she thought, going from dark to light, with maybe an accent wall of a contrasting color. Or maybe a warm, light gray with one dark-pink wall. Andrea was enjoying herself, and she was still getting used to it.

Next door, Emilio walked in circles. He was trying to comprehend why such a lovely woman would make such an enormous offer to a nobody like him, a dishwasher and some-times table server. Then he reminded himself that in Brazil, he was a teacher. He played music, and he had a daughter who had just taken her first steps. He'd seen it minutes ago on Skype. In the end, it was watching his daughter, missing her so terribly, and wanting so much for her that made up his mind. He would say yes to the kindly lovely woman. They would say the words and be married in name only, and he

would try very…very hard not to fall in love with her. And if
he did, he would make sure she never ever found out.

THE FOLLOWING MORNING, after the children had left for
school, Emilio called Andrea and asked if she wasn't busy,
could they talk about what she had offered the night before?

"Of course. Come over right now. I'm just about to start a
fresh pot of coffee. I'll make it extra strong the way you like it.
I can always add water to mine."

"I be right there. I have answer for you."

"Actually, could you give me ten minutes? I just got out of
the shower."

The coffee was still dripping through the filter when she
heard a soft knock at the back door. She'd already set out two
mugs on the kitchen table. On the way to the door, she ran
her fingers through her hair, doing her best to smooth the
still-damp spikes and swirls that seemed to sprout overnight to
fill in the bald patch. "Come in, come in. The coffee's almost
ready. Do you want some toast or something?"

Emilio held up his hand. "No, no. Tha's all right. I have
breakfast already."

Andrea pointed to a seat and to the two mugs on
the table.

"Take a seat, and pick out a mug."

He sat down and chose a dark-green mug with a frog on
it. Andrea filled it to the brim. She remembered he drank his
coffee black. After filling her own cup and adding a generous
splosh of hot water to tone it down, she took the chair across
from him.

"Well, are we getting married or not?" She flashed a
bright smile, trying to relax the man who was fiddling with his
mug and over-stirring his black coffee.

Emilio nodded and with some hesitancy, returned the smile.

"I think a lot about this. You are a very good woman. Very kind. Last night, I Skype my family. My little girl is walking now. If I marry you, I can bring her here. So, yes. I don' know how to thank you for this, but yes."

Andrea waved it away. "It's something I can do. And even if you hadn't stopped that man from possibly killing me, I would have done it anyway. You are a good man yourself, and you are working so hard. I would like to meet your daughter here in America. So…" She reached out her hand. "I guess it's a deal."

"Deal?" He extended his own hand and took hers.

"Deal, it means we both say yes."

"Deal!"

"After we finish our coffee, I think we should call your immigration lawyer and Reverend Olympia. If anyone in the world is going to marry us, it's going to be her."

"Deal!" said Emilio, still holding on to her hand.

43

E*arly February.*
    We are in the midst of a fierce snowstorm, and thus I have ample time to write because no one in possession of a sound mind would venture out of doors in the likes of this.

    The deed is done. I have sold Louisa's house, and the money I have realized from the sale will go far in assisting me in my journey south to locate and find Lottie's daughter.

    Poor Lottie is overjoyed at the prospect, and even though the Emancipation Proclamation is now law of the land, she still fears returning to the land of her bondage. So the task has fallen to me. Or more precisely, I have taken it on. Susan has offered to accompany me because it is not easy or safe for women to travel such a distance alone. Richard would gladly accompany me, but I think it best that he stay in Brookfields and be of assistance to Nathan, Lottie, and the children.

    This, of course, required my telling them all the true state of our, for appearances only, marriage. When I finished the tale, Nathan, Susan, and Lottie fell into fits of laughter. I realized then, it was the very first time I had heard our Lottie laugh aloud. I do believe she has finally come to trust us.

    More anon....LFW

Olympia closed the diary and placed it on the table next to her coffee cup as her phone rang. It was Andrea, asking her if she might possibly be free to perform a wedding that weekend—or maybe tomorrow if they could get the judge to waive the three-day waiting period.

44

I n the late afternoon of the following day, a select group of people stood waiting and fidgeting in the church office. Mrs. B., part of the happy conspiracy, had been asked to occupy the twins out of earshot in the children's area while the marriage of convenience was performed.

The bride wore jeans and a flannel shirt, the groom, a flannel shirt and jeans. Jim and Frederick served as the two witnesses, and Olympia deliberately did not "suit-up" in her clerical garb for the occasion. All present took care to observe the event with none of the traditional wedding language and as impersonally and perfunctorily as was possible. This was an arrangement...a contract—a marriage not a wedding.

If the bride was slightly dewy eyed and the groom was nervous,

no one made mention of it. It was a momentous event, in that, through the kindness and generosity of a good woman, a good man would be given the opportunity to realize a cherished dream for himself and his daughter.

At Emilio's insistence, all eight of them, the kids, and Mrs. B. went off to The Windjammer for a non-wedding supper.

He assured them that the manager would give him a special price, and it was his way of saying thank you.

What happened in the days to come would be anyone's guess. Or maybe it wouldn't. Not a one of them had missed the unspoken bond of affection growing between the not-bride and the not-groom. But were they simply two lost souls thrown together by unfortunate circumstance, who decided to weather the storm together? Or was there something happening that even the not-bride and not-groom were aware of or were unwilling to admit?

Frederick was willing to lay odds that sometime in the future, his lady-wife might well be called upon to tie a second and more permanent knot. A thought, for the time being, he kept to himself.

MID-FEBRUARY 1866

Spring is not far off now, the season of hope. I have not taken pen to paper in these precious pages for almost two months because all of my writing efforts have been entirely dedicated to locating Lottie's daughter. It took several letters and more than a few telegraphs—oh the wonder of invention—to locate where she might be. Lottie told us that before she escaped she was given word that her daughter had been sold to the Tucker family in nearby Amelia County, Virginia.

Armed with this scrap of information and a description of a light-skinned child with soft brown curls and blue eyes, I wrote letters, contacted people who knew people, and persevered until I believe I have located her. I must say that the Quakers have been invaluable in their help and with active abolitionist network of sympathetic citizens. Thus prepared, Susan and I will be off within the week.

I sometimes ask myself why I involve myself in such challenging undertakings, and the answer is always the same: I must because it is who I am. But there is an additional reason. Jonathan's father was a Minister of the Word and Christian deed. Perhaps this is my way of teaching his child about his father and his father's beliefs. The day is coming when he will ask about his father, and when that day comes, I will tell him the truth.

Meanwhile, there is a little girl in Virginia who, with God's help, (and mine) will soon be reunited with her mother.

More anon.....LFW.

EXCERPT FROM A TWISTED MISSION

Want more Olympia?
Want to start at the beginning?
Here is an excerpt from the very first in the Olympia Brown
Mystery series.

Chapter One

Without warning the snake slashed and zigzagged across the path just inches from his feet. He almost stepped on it. With his heart racing and sweat breaking out everywhere, he watched as the moving grasses off to his right indicated the direction of the reptile's speedy escape.

He straightened up and looked around to see if anyone had witnessed the incident but saw no one. He was morbidly afraid of snakes and had been since the day his father, drunk and trying to make a man of him, threw one in his face and then laughed when he screamed, fell on the ground and wet himself. The only thing he feared more than snakes these days was someone finding out about it. This was a close call, but so far his luck was holding. No one saw it. His shameful secret was still safe. When his breathing and heart rate returned to normal, he continued walking along the sandy path toward the crew shack. To be on the safe side, he stamped his feet, flapped his arms and made as much noise and commotion as he could.

Chapter Two

Across the street and up the short hill from the camp ground, a painfully thin and desperately unhappy young man scribbled a few words on a scrap of paper, folded it in half and pushed it deep into his jeans pocket. Then he climbed up on top of the battered old wooden dresser next to his bed. Careful to keep his balance, he tossed one end of a twisted sheet up and over the ceiling beam directly above him. He knotted it, yanked on it to test its strength and then secured it. Once that was done, he tied the other end around his neck. He had taken great care with the measurements so that when jumped off and kicked the shoddy dresser away from beneath him, his feet would not reach the floor. He hoped, even dared to pray, it would be quick.

Chapter Three

A fiftieth birthday, whatever else it might be, is a milestone. It can be a warning signal, a turning point or both. It can be loudly celebrated or quietly ignored, but it cannot be denied. It is a time when many will choose to step back and take stock. The Rev. Dr. Olympia Brown had just reached that significant event with as many questions in her mind as she had years logged onto the calendar. The two at the very top of the list were, should she continue as a college chaplain and professor of humanities and religion at Merriwether College, or should she change direction, leave academia and take on a full time parish ministry?

On the nonprofessional and more personal front there were more questions. Now that her two sons, Malcolm and Randall, were technically out of the safe suburban nest, her status as a not-very-swinging single was lonely. Maybe she should be more proactive about creating a little more action in that corner of her life. Maybe she should move out of her white, middle class, three-bedroom expanded cape in the town with the good schools that she needed when the boys were young and buy a condo in Boston or Cambridge. That would certainly ease her commute and save money on gas.

She could take her mother's advice, let nature take its course and wait for the universe to reveal what the future might offer—but Olympia rarely took her mother's advice, so she eliminated that one even before she wrote it down. And so it was on a spectacular summer day in early June, she was sitting in her back yard, sipping iced tea and making a list … or maybe it was a five-year plan—she hadn't decided which. In big block letters she created three columns across the top of the sheet of paper: Done, Yet to be done, and Wishful thinking bucket list.

If nothing else, and there was a whole lot of else, Olympia Brown was methodical and well organized. She typically set reasonable goals for herself and then in her own determined fashion strategized how to reach them. At age fifty, she knew who she was and pretty much what she wanted out of life. She also knew what she was and was not prepared give up in order to bring that about, or so she thought.

However, nothing that was about to happen in the coming summer was on this list and no one, not even Olympia, the practical plotter, could have predicted or planned for what did happen. She couldn't possibly know it, but it seemed she was at the mercy of a host of gods and goddesses who were bored and decided to have a bit of fun. The object of their ungodly mischief of fancy and foolishness was a middle-aged, slightly restless college professor who in one unguarded moment said she might be ready for a change. She looked again at the sheet of paper in her lap, made a face, and scrawled, "None of the above." Then she crumpled the paper and tossed back and high over her shoulder.

She decided to take a second look at the invitation she'd received to be a summer chaplain at Orchards Cove in Maine. A summer of fresh sea air and camping under towering pines in a seaside village would be a refreshing change and give her plenty of time to think about her future. Would it not?

Olympia's mother also told her, "Be careful what you wish for." It would have been good advice, had she listened, but she didn't, and therein hangs the tale.

ABOUT THE AUTHOR

(Rev. Dr.) Judith Campbell is a Unitarian Universalist Community-based minister. In addition to the Olympia Brown Mysteries, she has published poetry, children's books, two books on watercolor painting, and articles on religion, spirituality and the arts. She lives by the ocean in Plymouth, Massachusetts, with her English husband, Chris, (who bears a striking resemblance to Frederick), and their two cats. Writing is her passion, her challenge and most authentic way she can live into her ministry.

Judith is available in person or on SKYPE to speak to your book group or at your library. As a minister and teacher, she is available to lead workshops and retreats on fiction, memoir and spiritual biography.

Please contact her and get on her mailing list through her website, or through her Facebook page, Judith Campbell Author. She loves to hear from her readers, and will respond personally to every email.

For more information
www.judithcampbell-holymysteries.com
revdocmom@comcast.net

ALSO BY JUDITH CAMPBELL